THE BIRD CATCHER
AND OTHER STORIES

For my father

Because of him I never learned how to be a perfected woman

ISBN: 978-1-937543-75-4

This book is also available in electronic book format.

Hasanat, Fayeza

The Birdcatcher and Other Stories / Hasanat

CONTENTS

Chapter 1: The White Room

The office was full of horses. White clay, marble, stone, ceramic horses—standing by the door and hanging on the wall. All white. The chair at the center of the room, the L-shaped desk, and the gigantic Mac screen. White. The sofa in the corner, the stylish water cooler, the vase and all the flowers in it, the rug underneath, and the center table. White. The therapist sat on her white leather chair wearing her white teeth that dazzled like a set of pearls on her pale pink gums, behind her Tom Ford lips. Wasn't that a Tom Ford she was wearing? Or was it the new Rouge Volupté Shine? Whichever it was, her lips were the only non-white element in the whole room—or in her possession. Why was she in need of such a brave color? Did she want me to look at her lips when I talked? Shouldn't I be aiming for her ears? Shouldn't I be the one wearing that Volupté Shine since I'd be doing most of the talking?

I sank into the white sofa and realized that I was too brown and not properly dressed. My skin was dry and my hair smelled of sand. As I tried to smooth my frizzed hair with my palms, my right elbow hit something hard. It was a file board that he was holding. Was he still filling out those forms? What information was he scribbling in? The color of my vomit? The last time he relaxed inside me?

The pearls that were her teeth finally turned her smiles into words and asked him to leave the room.

"But I'm a doctor myself," he exploded. "She's my wife, and I have every right!!!"

"She's my patient now, and I would like you to leave."

He gave me a reassuring smile. Was his nose always this crooked? Goodness! I had spent my whole adult life with this man and never noticed he had a meandering nose! What was I, blind?

"Do you know what brought you here?"

And his ears? What big ears he got! Better to—how did that saying go? Oh, I remember, better to hear... hear what? What did he hear? What?

"WHAT?"

"Why are you here?"

"Doctor's order."

"Why did the doctors want you to be evaluated by me?"

"Because I walked into the ocean."

"Why?"

What is wrong with this woman? Why is she so paradisally dumb? Is that even a word? Paradise—paradise-al—paradisally— it could easily work as an effective adjective for her. Angelic is a good option, too. Dumb, white-attired angel, with white halo and wings. This angel's halo is her white horse murals and paintings... and those teeth that were once pearls... I wanted to find the pearls that were once my eyes; and unlike you, I know what I have lost, and I know where to find them! That's WHY, bitch.

"I wanted to feel the ocean."

"Do you know how to swim?"

"Nope."

"What if you drowned?"

"That is the point."

"What is?"

"Drowning. Oceans can't drown an already drowned woman."

"When did you drown?"

"I don't know. I only wanted to wade through the ocean and never return. And I hate him for pulling me away from it. But it doesn't matter though; there's still time."

"What did you say?"

"I said I'll take that walk another day. Do you know the Bengali word for ocean? Shamudra. Don't you just love the sound of that word? To shamudra I will go. You think you can stop me? I don't think so. Ocean is the home where I will return."

"Do you know what you're saying?"

"Don't you?"

"Mrs. Can-de-cahr, do you really mean what you're saying? I'm sorry if I'm repeating myself, but I have to ask—to make sure."

"Yeah, yeah, I know. Everyone wants to be sure of my safety—even those who don't know my name and can't say the name that was never mine. What safety? I've lived on the land for too long and now I'm yearning for water. I want to walk into the ocean to—"

"Kill yourself?"

"Whatever."

"And you're saying you'll try it again?"

"Maybe; of course. I'm not sure why not."

This angelic white train of talks! How long does she think she can run her mouth like this? And she gets paid for this? Evaluate? Holy shit! E-valu-ate. Ate what? My ocean. My freedom. These parasitical omnivores—getting paid for gorging everything—hope, dream, love, desire, laughter, life. And I'm the one being evaluated. Bullshit!

"Where are you going? Mrs. Can-de-cahr, please come

back and take your seat. Sit down."

You sit down! You fucking sit down on your fucking ass and keep looking at your fucking fake horses. I am done sitting.

"No, thank you, I don't need to sit. Because I know what your plans are. Please ask your nurses to let go of me. I don't want to sleep. No!"

"I am sorry, Mrs. Can-de-cahr. But this medicine will help you."

"Oh, and look what you've done! You have turned me into a watercolor painting, and now I am washing off."

"I am sorry, Dr. Can-de-cahr."

Who is that? Which of the horses is talking now? Those were horses that were men—strong, cruel. Man. Where are they taking me now? To my ocean?

"Your wife isn't safe anywhere else. We have to keep her under supervision for a while."

Bedlam . . . Belmont . . . who went to Bedlam, Anne? Was it you? Or was it Sylvia? Oh Robert, don't take me to a maison de santé . . . Let me go back to my home, to the ocean . . . to shamudra I will go . . .

"It's a good facility and she will get proper treatment. Don't worry, Dr. Can-de-cahr, your wife will come back to you, fresh and cured."

Oh, I wish I could fly out of my head, but that is out of the question now.

Chapter 2: The Naming Game

Back home, we used to play this game called musical chairs, in which neither the chairs nor the players got to play their own music. All we had to do was walk around a bunch of chairs. Someone would put on some music and we would walk around the chairs as long as the music played. We had to claim a chair the moment the music stopped. Once safely seated, we laughed at the fool who stood alone and chair-less.

The people in the room that day—sitting in a semicircle, listening to Rampal's flute—seemed to be playing musical chairs. I sat on a chair that wore my nametag. The name wasn't my own, but I sat down anyway. The room was dark and twelve people were listening to Rampal, waiting for a signal to start their game. The conductor of the game stood in front of the group. He was taller than my eyes, and he was hiding a borrowed smile underneath his red mustache. I instantly knew from whom he borrowed the smile. Those were teeth that were her pearls! It's like a set of generic dentures—this fake smile of theirs—all they do is switch it from one mouth to another! I wondered how that woman in white was managing her calm, now that her smile was gone.

The girl sitting next to me looked straight at me after she finished eating all her nails. Was she planning to eat mine? I tucked my hands in my cardigan pocket. Can't take that risk. The one on my other side was checking out the gentleman sitting four chairs away from her. The man was shaking his legs as if they were car wheels stuck under piles of snow and he had to take them out to get them going.

"My name is Dr. Sean O'Sullivan," the conductor creaked, "and I'll be your counselor for the next two weeks. You are advised to strictly follow all the rules of this institution. No phone calls. No sharp objects; no unsupervised strolls inside or outside the vicinity. You will sleep in a room of two, with your lights on, and your clothes on, of course. No sex, no drugs, no alcohol. Just life. You will gather here in this room every morning after breakfast. You'll talk about your fears and frustrations, and you'll write daily journals or letters addressing the persons or issues that dragged you here.

You will have an hour-long yoga and a thirty-minute Zumba class; one-hour music session, one-hour manual labor in the garden, one hour chit-chat after lunch, and three hours of TV after dinner; then fifteen minutes of strolling in our beautiful moon garden before you'll call it a night. And in two weeks' time, you'll become a totally different person—jumping with joy. Now, let's hear your names and your reasons for being here. Who wants to start?"

Ah! He walked straight from morning to madness. And this name telling game! As if it would solve all the problems— as if the secret is in our names—as if our names are our beginnings and our ends, the poison and the antidote. My name is the climax, and my reason, its grand finale.

"Hi, I am Rhonda. Sorry, I bite my nails when I'm nervous. I'm here because I tried to kill myself after my stepfather raped me."

What, you all are just going to sit there and sigh? Didn't you hear what she just said? Are you afraid to lose your musical chair if you stand up and give her a hug? Okay, I'll go.

"Can we please stay in our seats until everyone is done introducing themselves?"

There you go again—through the shit-hole of rules. You want to kill yourself? Fine, wait in line. You want to report a rape? Sorry, out of rape-kits. Just wash it off and take a morning-after pill. Don't worry, it's just sex; consider it an adventurous experience. Like one of those fifty shades of fucking gray.

"Hi, I am Jason. I'm here because I failed to end my life—and that was my third attempt, man!"

What a pathetic loser you are, but don't you worry. Fourth time will be the charm. Failure makes the pillar of death.

"Hi, I'm Rita. I'm a sex-aholic and I tried to jump off of the apartment when my boyfriend refused to—"

So that's why you were checking out the leg-shaker? But why is it that you're the one who wanted to jump? It should be your boyfriend who should have jumped. What kind of a man doesn't want to have sex multiple times in one night? Poor Rita, you've chosen a wrong friend for a boy-toy. You should've found yourself some meek Bengali men—the ones that meow like cats, but fancy themselves as Royal Bengal Tigers in bed, because their secret hair frizzes up like whiskers, and because the lights are out.

"Hi, I am Andrew. I'm here because I told my Calculus teacher that I would kill her one day."

"Hi, I'm Caroline. I'm here because . . ."

"I am Morrhene. I'm here . . ."

"Hi, I am . . ."

What is this? Association of self-loathing? Why am I listening to all this bullshit?

"Mrs. Kan-de-car, I mean, Mrs. Khan-dekar, would you please sit down?"

"I want to leave this room."

"I'm afraid that's not possible. Sit down and tell us your name."

"My name? Don't you know that already? Didn't you give me this nametag that hangs around my neck, like an albatross?"

"I am sorry, what now?"

"Albatross! Coleridge, *Ancient Mariner*! Never mind."

"Please introduce yourself."

"Fine. Hi, I am, look at this name, not Can-de-Cahr, or Kan-de-car, or Khan-dekar. It's Mrs. Khandakar. Do you know how to say it now? Excellent. Now, can I go?"

"I'm sorry, but we want to know your first name."

"Which one?"

"How many you got?"

"Too many."

"Well, then, let's hear them all."

"My name is Nirjhara, a Bengali word, and I was named so by my father; my mother named me Labonyo; my grandmother named me Chandora, because I was born during a full moon; my grandfather named me Ameera, for I needed a Muslim name; my mother's mother named me Durba, meaning grass; and my husband named me Ranji's mother, for that's who I was to him—his daughter's mother. But if you ask me, I would have very much loved to bear a name like Kadombori, Kadombini, or Sylvia; Virginia, Lizzy, Anne, or at least Edna."

And now you are playing dead? No reaction? No ahhhs and ooohs and awwws and sighs and gasps? Come on, don't pretend like you have seen too many brown skins here and you are familiar with their multiple first names.

"I'm a woman married to a house. Oh, and I am here because I wanted to walk into the ocean, and I'm telling you, I'll do that the day I get out of here."

"You mean you wanted to end your life."

"No, Dr. O'Sullivan, I mean I wanted to walk right into the ocean. After all, this is Florida. Aren't we surrounded by oceans? Isn't it a typical Floridian's dream to walk into one?"

"You mean, to walk by."

"Whatever you say, but I know my prepositions."

Life is all about right word choices, right verbs, and

right prepositions. If you walk by the ocean, you are a lover of life. If you walk into it out of your love for the ocean, you are kept here as a prisoner until you learn the correct use of prepositions.

"Nirjhurr... Lebanani—I mean Mrs. Can-de-cahr, please calm down. Sit down, please! We'll take a break now. Nurse! Nurse! Everyone, let's take a coffee break. We'll start our letter-writing session in the afternoon. Nirajh-Rujha, I mean Ke-dumb-ri, I mean Durban ... Damn it, can I call you Edna?"

Chapter 3: The Letters

Day 1

If writing solved all troubles, then why am I here? These people, those people, them, all, you! None of you can handle the idea of an uncharted territory of thoughts inside one's head. You have to read the words so that you can unclothe their meanings. You always want to know, as if knowing is the ultimate erotic pleasure. You want to impregnate all the unborn thoughts resting cozily inside the cranial womb of a *lazy laughing languid* woman. Reading my letters will make you stronger, I know. But what good will it do for me? Will it cure my ocean-lust?

Day 2

How should I start this unwilling letter? Should I address you as Dear—dear what? Dear Husband of mine? Dear Man? My dear Ranji's papa?

Dear Mr. Can-de-cahr . . . Can you please drive de cahr toward the ocean? I need to breathe.

"How's the writing going, Edna?"

"My writing isn't going anywhere, Dr. O'Sullivan. It doesn't have legs."

"You Indian people, you're so funny, hahahaha."

"Dr. O'Sullivan, you Irish people are funny too!"

"I'm not Irish, my lady; my ancestors were, but I am 100 percent American."

"I'm NOT Indian."

"No? You surely don't have Indian accent, but your long wavy hair confused me. Married to an Indian then?"

"Nope; we're from Bangladesh."

"I see! What exactly is your geographical location?"

"It's a tiny island, stuck between Thailand and Indonesia, almost close to Japan, and not far from Australia."

"Sounds like a perfect vacation spot."

Thirty years. I have lived in this country for thirty years, and still haven't found a way to drill into these people's heads the concept of my existence as someone not-Indian-now, but once was. So I dismantle your diminishing knowledge of world geography every time people like you ask me the location of a country that is not even my country anymore. Next time you ask me the same question, I will give your imagination a run and shift my beloved island to Antarctica, and you wouldn't know. When is the last time anyone asked you where Ireland is? Dumb shrink!

Day 3

Should I give you a name, husband? Should we do a game of role-playing? It always flares up the sex, you once told me, when you wanted me to dress up as a maid, like the ones you've seen in a plotless porn. But this is not a sexy game I'm asked to play. I can't wear a funky white cap and spread my body as a blank slate for you to write on with that pen of yours that dangles like a monkey's mushy banana in a bristly jungle. This

Day 8

Do you know that the only friend I had was a tree? Didn't you see me standing by the big weeping willow in the backyard, holding its stooping branches as if they were strands of Rapunzel's sad hair? Didn't you see my lips whispering songs at its leafy ears?

Of course you couldn't see, for the bright sun had gouged out your eyes years ago.

Husband, are you the poisonous tree that broods over my tombstone?

Day 9

I am most sorrowful in June, my very own rainy season. June is when raindrops run through every pore of my skin and turn me into a weeping willow. If the sky was under my feet and it poured from beneath, my rainy season would then sink inside me and grow like an unfathomable sea.

Day 10

Do you remember a time when we sat together and sipped our afternoon tea and laughed, talking about silly and unimportant things?

Neither do I.

Day 11

Remember when I told you how I would love to play my violin, sitting by the ocean and overlooking all your intolerable fusses—your irritable bowel, irascible stomach, kiwi allergy and cantaloupe intolerance?

How would you remember things you were never told?

Day 12

Once you told me I was lucky to have nothing missing in my life. "How many women from our part of the world do you think have all that you have? What wouldn't they do to live your life! There is nothing missing in your life, nothing!"

Husband, you were right. There is NOTHING.

Day 13

You always gave me everything I needed. Safety, security, happiness. A paid-off house and a solid retirement fund. Social Security benefits once we became senior citizens. Proper medical care in our old age. Two adjacent burial spots—bought in advance—in the Muslim cemetery by the mosque; everything is ready and waiting. All we have to do is live the American Dream and die like true Muslims.

Husband, I wish you knew that we've been in our graves all our lives.

Day 14

We outgrow everything: a mother's womb, the skin that clothes us, the masks that hide our pains , words that contain our thoughts; and sometimes, we outgrow love.

Husband, you said you loved me the most the day I bore you two sons. You called them your twin projects and promised to raise them like a dream—your dream. That day, your eyes glowed the most with lust for love and greed for life. I lay dead in the hospital bed, thinking of the victor, Frankenstein. And I outgrew love.

I was brave once and I too knew how to dance. But twenty-five years ago, on that day, you made me aware of my missing feet: the ones you had replaced with a mermaid tail.

"I do not thank you for your mercy, Mr. Robert Audley, for I know exactly what it is worth."

"What's that?"

"Something I read years ago."

"Oh, you and your Indian humor!"

"Dr. O'Sullivan, what do I do with these letters?"

"I can keep them in your file; but don't come back to write the sequel."

"Don't worry, I won't."

"By the way, Edna, what's that you wrote at the end of your last letter? Look, here: ***ajh-amai- she-mad-ri —ja-bou—***"

"That's written in Bengali, my native language. It reads, ***Aaj ami shamudre jabo.***"

"What does it mean?"

"*To Shamudra, I will go.* It means I'm going home today."

BRIDE
OF THE
VANISHING SUN

Aandhi's grandmother always said that Aandhi's eyes were wider than a gazelle's and prettier than the rays of the morning sun—if properly decked with *kajal*. She stealthily looked at the possessed man with her gazelle eyes and watched him dive into the dessert tray.

The possessed man finished every item, piece by piece, put the roses aside, petal by petal, licked his fingers one by one, and wiped his mouth, crease by crease, with a white handkerchief offered to him by Aandhi—who still stood there like a confused deer, trying to anticipate every move of the seventeen huntsmen and a prospective groom. To her surprise, the huntsmen said nothing, and it was the possessed man who delivered her fate in a loud and clear voice. "Let's go, uncles and brothers," he told his companions once he was done with the dessert plate, "I am full and sleepy, and this woman is very dark—like...like...Bholi, our black cow. I can't marry a Bholi. Never!"

They marched out, leaving Aandhi behind, like the shadow of a lonely black cow with dark, deep eyes, grazing in an empty room.

"We should've arranged for a lunch party," Abdur Rahman later said. "She would've looked prettier in broad daylight."

"I told you, we should have taken her to Aunt Lily's house in the city," the second of the seven brothers said. "No one could have detected her complexion under the bright city lights."

"Or, you could have arranged for an evening session as I suggested," commented their grandmother. "A dark woman looks fair under the evening sun."

"It's not Aandhi's fault. These lanterns don't produce sufficient light. Even I can't see my own hands under this light," Sufia muttered, waving her flawlessly fair hands in the air. Her words were ignored by her sons, just like the last rays of the vanishing sun that were being disregarded by the approaching darkness of a night that fell short in covering the stain of humiliation from Aandhi's face.

Two years later, when Abdur Rahman was preparing to throw a lunch party for another prospective groom's family, both his mother and grandmother strongly opposed him.

"Let them see Aandhi in the evening," said his mother.

"Let the twilight play its magic on her face, and I promise you won't be disappointed," the grandmother implored.

Abdur Rahman felt agitated. He had been hopelessly searching for a suitable groom for Aandhi. From morning till sundown, he never had a minute to stop worrying. Abdur Rahman had to quit college to take over family responsibilities after his father's death, and he had been playing the role of guardian for his nine siblings ever since. He never had time to look back. At thirty-six, he had acquired the wrinkles of a sixty-year-old man. As he sat there listening to his mother and grandmother's whimsical ideas, Abdur Rahman felt cornered. He rubbed his palm over his forehead—frantically trying to erase the wrinkles as he listened to them. At one point, just to put an end to the ceaseless argument, Abdur Rahman decided to surrender to the whims of the two elderly women.

"I will invite them for tea," he said, "but make sure to keep it like that. Prepare simple refreshments and some tea only. We will feed them a hearty dinner if the bridal viewing goes well and once the wedding takes place—and I'll make sure the wedding takes place right away—tonight, if possible!"

He gave orders to set the tables in the northwest corner of the rose garden. The fierce sun stood in the middle of the sky, right on top of Abdur Rahman's head, generating anger that broke like sweat and ran like a stream of frustration over his balding head and wrinkled face. If this plan did not work, nothing would, and he did not know how to face his mother if the setting sun did not perform its desired task that evening. He supervised the workers as they made sitting arrangements for the guests, placed bouquets of freshly cut flowers on each table, and brought in refreshments. Like a guard dog, Abdur Rahman stood there, watching his workmen transform an empty yard into a magical spot.

The guests arrived in the afternoon. The groom's uncles munched on the sweetened rice balls and fried cauliflower, the groom chewed on his nails, and the father kept on twisting the head of his fountain pen on a notebook in a futile attempt to figure out the financial situation of this seemingly tight-fisted family. Twilight fell and the future bride was summoned to serve tea. This time, Aandhi's grandmother had made her wear a yellow sari. Earlier in the morning, Aandhi was given a raw turmeric treatment. Her whole body was covered with turmeric paste and she was ordered to sit still for two hours in a dark room so that her dark skin could absorb some of the orange tinge from the turmeric paste. The paste was supposed to brighten her skin tone, and the yellow sari was meant to add some more radiance to the turmeric-treated skin. Most importantly, there was twilight—the time that was neither day nor dusk and embraced both day and night. Twilight is the time when the sun prepares for his magnificent departure while flirting one last time with the enticing earth that eagerly waits to be embraced by night's darkness. Twilight is when exit meets entrance and mystifies the yearning of time present for time future. But Aandhi's grandmother was not bothered by any philosophical implications of such a mating of fleeting moments. All that she cared about was her granddaughter's future. She wanted to make sure that neither the vanishing sun nor the darkening earth stole the light from Aandhi's face.

"Today is my Aandhi's day," she said, and she gave order to her grandsons to make twilight stand still and work its magic.

Aandhi's hair was not braided this time. Her grandmother had brushed it with jasmine oil and tucked a few marigolds on the right side of Aandhi's face, just above her ear. She put the *anchal* of the yellow sari over Aandhi's head and carefully pinned it on her hair, tugging it behind the marigolds. "This time, you don't go clumsy by pulling your *anchal* off and showing your bare head to those strangers," she warned as she pushed Aandhi out to the backyard. Sufia watched over everything with her two cautious eyes. She took her regular seat by the window from where she could see the whole backyard. She did not blink for a moment as Aandhi stepped out of the room and walked toward the garden where a handful of strange men flocked to give their verdict on her appearance. The groom looked at Aandhi for a moment and then went back to his usual nail biting habit; the uncles scrutinized the girl from all possible angles, trying to determine the exact shade of her skin tone.

"Don't look away!" Sufia wanted to scream. *"Her eyes are dark and deep; her lips curve the prettiest of smiles; unruly ringlets hang over her smooth forehead. Long, black hair floats like clouds. If she looked at you, you would feel a strange emotion taking over your heart; you might have the urge to look back as she softly walks away. Oooh, look, look, look at my beautiful girl as she bends her head slightly like a fawn and offers herself for this sacrifice...."* But Sufia's ceaseless thoughts never reached the groom and his men because they were deaf to her truth. She sat like a framed picture by the window and watched a group of strangers playing chess with her daughter's fate. Like a painting of a sorrow, she sat there, waiting for the decree to be delivered by some men who might never understand the pains of motherhood.

The groom's father looked at Abdur Rahman. "She is unusually dark. Very, very dark. My son is a white sahib compared to her."

"I apologize for my sister's limitations," said Abdur Rahman, in a dry tone.

"My son is going to college to get his bachelor's. He plans to be a Civil Servant for the East Pakistan Government."

"*Mashallah*," murmured Abdur Rahman.

"But, you see, he does not realize that I am just a poor school teacher."

"We will bear all the expenses of his education," said Abdur Rahman, in a confident voice.

"You see, I have six other children and my house is made of corrugated tin. Winters are too cold and summers are too stormy in our part of the village. Your sister might not be comfortable living there."

"We will build you a brick house." Abdur Rahman declared.

"My second son is studying for a medical degree, whose tuition I am unable to pay."

"Don't worry about his expenses, sir," Abdur Rahman's voice was desperate.

"I don't even have money to prepare for this wedding ceremony," the groom's father said meekly.

"In that case, the wedding will take place tonight. I am sending for the marriage registrar right now," Abdur Rahman said..

When the wedding ceremony was over, Sufia sat in the lonely garden, wrapped in the darkness of an autumn night, thinking of her daughter's bright smile and sparkling eyes. "Why didn't they admire her beauty?" She asked her mother-in-law, "didn't they see how pretty she is?"

"They didn't, because they can't," replied the old woman. "When was the last time you saw a man with a good eyesight? They are just a bunch of opportunist men, and men usually see what they want to see."

That night, Aandhi found herself married to a nail-biting youth named Nizam, who did not have the eyes to appreciate the magic of the evening sun.

Chapter Two

For Aandhi, cooking was a creative work that took a lot of vision and confidence. She found catering a hassle, especially for an aggressive crowd whose hunger depended not on the beauty of food but on the target subject they were coming to inspect. In a bridal inspection party, dinner was nothing but appetizer, and the prospective bride was treated as the main entrée. Aandhi had to make sure the appetizer round went well before the entrée—which, in this case, was her second daughter Shila—entered the scene. She wanted to offer them rich, savory, traditional food to send the message that they could afford to pay proper respect to any potential groom—irrespective of his status and class. Aandhi therefore had been very busy throughout the week, making sure that the caterer followed her instructions in meticulous details.

"Make sure you garnish that pilaf with plenty of raisins and walnuts. The chicken curry that's going to go over the pilaf must be cooked with fresh yogurt, nutmeg, and cinnamon. The kabobs should be well done, but don't make them crunchy. And for the dessert—" Her wrinkled brow evened a little when the caterer promised to strictly follow her instructions. "These people," she complained to her daughters, "these people are playing with my temper. Can you believe they almost forgot to deep fry the walnuts and onion rings in clarified butter? You pay them loads of money to cook such simple dishes and yet they mess up."

"Why don't you cook yourself if you are so worried?" her daughter, Shila, asked. "And who cares how the food looks? You can't fix my flaws by serving them flawless food. Why don't you learn to—" Kheya jumped in and dragged Shila away from the room.

"What's wrong with you?" Kheya hissed at her older sister. "You are already in trouble for refusing to follow her plan, don't you know?"

"So what?" Shila retorted. "I refuse to be served on a gold platter, like your freaking authentic biryani dish, Mother!"

"Don't make me open my mouth, Shila," Aandhi screamed from the other room, "You go to college not to learn that women's rights stuff. A college-educated girl gets a better husband, and that's all there is. A girl's only rightful right is to make a good wife when schooling is done!"

Aandhi was angry—not with Shila, but with the whole world and especially at her neighbor's dark-skinned girl, who recently got married to an engineer and moved to California. And here she was, stuck in a tunnel of torment, trying to appease a defiant daughter who did not understand the magnitude of the misfortune imprinted on her skin! Aandhi was somewhat lucky with her first daughter, Rima, who now lived in New York with her husband. Granted, the marriage was not a good one, but so what? At least she gave her something to brag about when she moved to America. Which Bangladeshi mother in her sane mind would not feel proud of a daughter living in the city that never slept? Aandhi was no exception. She always made sure that her pride did not go unnoticed by the ambitious mothers of her community.

"Rima sent me this," Aandhi would casually say whenever she had the chance of showing off a new prized possession. As she talked, she would always clasp the prestigious gold monogram of the brand, hanging from the front zipper of her purse. "She told me, 'Mom, you have no idea how hard it was for me to go to 34th Street from where I live, just to go to the big Macy's building to get this purse. So, you must use it with care!' This is authentic, you see! She did not get it from China Town. She said, 'Ma, first I had to get into Q Train from 177th street; then I get down to 42nd and go to the other side of the station to take E train. It takes 40 minutes to reach 34th Street.' And if she wants to go to Jackson Heights to get some Bangla food, then she has to take F train from there...."

"Are these trains safe for our girls?" asked an inquisitive woman once.

"Don't be silly, sister! These are underground trains. They are faster than wind. Everyone is safe inside those trains, and yet nobody is. It's very dangerous to stand too close to a moving train because the magnetic power pulls you toward it like an iron shackle!"

As much as Aandhi's listeners were mesmerized by the way she depicted vivid details of a beautiful city she had never seen, her husband, Nizam, remained equally disillusioned. For Nizam, *opinion* and *choice* were words of male origin. For him, his older daughter's decision to marry a man of her choice was a matter of disgust. He saw it as a sign of the daughter's disobedience and the mother's failure. He considered Aandhi a failing mother, whose daughters moved about like a bunch of blind mice—with no sense of direction. Their oldest daughter, Rima, had run away with a man ten years her senior and now lived in some dingy, one-bedroom apartment somewhere in New York City, working as an interpreter for the county. The

man she had eloped with was a discontented dreamer who —
with a college degree in Bengali literature and no money in his
pocket—drove a cab through the endless roads of Manhattan
for countless hours, eating his meals while driving and using
empty water bottles as urinals. Nizam knew that Aandhi's
stories about Rima's happy life grew out of her cowardice to
face reality. Being aware of the distance between his older
daughter's truth and his wife's fiction, Nizam was adamant
not to let any worthless visions disrupt the fate of his other
daughters. To him, daughters were potted houseplants in need
of shade and constant care. He considered it his sacred duty
to nurture them well—until it was time to replant them in
suitable containers permanently. He was therefore unyielding
to the headstrong opinions of his younger daughters, Shila and
Kheya. Being the youngest in the family, Kheya was rebellious.
She was born to say "no" to every possible proposition and
would never take "no" for an answer to any of her own
demands. Nizam was intrigued by the way logic and anti-logic
worked simultaneously in Kheya's head. He never worried
about Kheya, because somehow he knew this headstrong
daughter of his possessed the willpower to turn and bend life
in any direction, at any given time. It was Shila who worried
him most. Shila shared her older sister's whims and her
mother's look. She had inherited Aandhi's slender figure, long
hair, deep eyes, and dark skin.

Shila wanted to marry Ronni—the man of her dreams,
the source of her life's joy, the spineless lover. Ronni was a
political science major, and Plato was his mentor. He was
always scared of people around him; he was even scared to
hold her hand in public. "When we marry, we will make love
all night long, but until then, we will live like two conquerors
of the temptations of flesh," he used to say. Shila never
questioned Ronni's meekness because she believed in him. But
when Shila desperately sought Ronni's help and asked him

to save her from the traps of an arranged marriage that her parents were planning for her, Ronni's meekness melted like ice. He stood before her like an awakened man. He reminded Shila of all the walls that stood between them: he was a rich man's only son, and she was still a girl too brown to be accepted by his parents. Ronni held her hand and kissed her lips, and then softly said, "My love for you is like a black rose that never fades or loses its color." He then slowly walked away and merged with the crowd, leaving Shila standing alone, like a damaged statue.

Shila was always aware of her dark complexion. She knew which colors went well with her skin, which shades of green faded against it, or which tinge of crimson fell flat. Her sister Rima always admired her radiantly smooth skin.

"You could have easily ousted the Queen of Sheba," Rima used to say. "How can you be so pretty?"

"Because mother loves me more," Shila always answered with pride.

Shila used to think that her beauty was the result of their mother's constant care. Since childhood, Aandhi always forced her to drink a glass of milk mixed with a spoon of turmeric paste. Another paste made from orange peel, turmeric, honey, and ground fenugreek seed was a regular part of her daily skin care. Shila thought she was given extra attention because she was prettier than her sisters. It was only recently she realized that her mother's extra care signified her lack of beauty—not the overabundance of it—and that the treasure she hid beneath her skin or within her heart did not matter to anyone—neither to Ronni nor to the families of all those prospective grooms who had rejected her because of the darkness she wore on her skin.

That day, in order to please her parents and appease her

fate, Shila agreed to cover her body with layers of turmeric paste. She sat hidden in a dark room for hours so the golden glow of the paste would obliterate her darkness. Her mother made her wear a yellow sari and her cousins took her to a beauty salon to fix her hair. She refused to put on any makeup, but no one listened. Without added color, she looked dull, they said. Shila had the most perfect smile in the family. "I don't need a candle in a dark night when the power is out," Nizam always said. "I only need my Shila to give me a big smile. Her beautiful bright teeth will then light up the room for me." And Ronni used to call her his own starless night. But her father did not oppose when Shila's smiles got buried under lustrous lipstick. And Ronni? He had already left in search of a bright day, because he was afraid of the dark.

The nicely decorated patio, with oval tables and cone-shaped vases filled with gardenias and Shasta daisies, waited eagerly for the "bridal viewing" scheduled to start at twilight. Shifat Alam, the prospective groom, was a short man with a big extended family. He was an established businessman, with his own garment factory and a promising future. Shifat Alam and his brothers lived in a four-story building centrally controlled by the patriarch—the elder Mr. Alam—who lived on the second floor. A man in his seventies, Mr. Alam was a powerful father. He used his walking stick—which he moved left and right, like a baton—to control the movement of all his sons. His sons paused or proceeded, following the direction of the stick, while the old man kept narrating the story of his happy household.

"I love to be surrounded by my family," he told Nizam. "I always make sure my children and grandchildren sit with me for every meal. They can live in separate houses as much as they want, but they have to gather around me three times a day and eat with me. It gives me a sense of immense gratification, you know, to be surrounded by my offspring."

Wearing a placid smile on his face, Nizam listened to
the stories of domestic joys of the Alam household, where the
father was the king and the mother was in charge of the kitchen.
In that house, the mother, Alam, distributed domestic chores
among her five daughters-in-law, allotting each of them an
assigned day to cook for the whole extended family. If Shila were
lucky enough to be a part of that household, she would also
have weekly assigned days to show off her culinary skills. The
elder Mr. Alam finally ended his tale admiring Nizam's authorial
role as a father of three daughters and commending Aandhi
for serving a grand dinner. He then expressed his eagerness to
meet the girl who might become his youngest daughter-in-law.
Aandhi left in haste. "Don't be nervous; they're just a bunch of
men," she told Shila. "Enter like a queen and dazzle them with
your presence before the sun goes dark."

From her room, Aandhi could see the horizontal
lines of pinkish golden rays at the end of the sky, glistening
through her window—as if framing for her a vibrant display
of hope—from one corner of the window to the other. She
could see Shila, standing in front of the elder Mr. Alam, clad
in a gorgeous yellow sari and adorned with jewelry made of
24-carat gold. Aandhi sprang to her feet and held her breath,
praying to the god of twilight to fulfill a mother's wish. On
the patio, Nizam sat like a guard dog, watching his daughter
serve coffee in a rhythmic pattern, tilt and pour and lift the
pot up, tilt and pour and lift the pot up: her ostinato of hope.
He observed how between each serving, amidst the clanking of
bangles and tinkling of coffee spoons, the thirsty men waited
in silence, like a pause: *Pause del Silenzio.*

The groom suddenly mumbled some words in a soft
voice. Startled, Shila thought he wanted more sugar in his
coffee. As she dipped the sugar spoon in his cup, his hand
touched hers. She recoiled, and he felt a flow of warmth

running through his veins. If only she were not this dark, he thought, the chemistry was sure to have worked between them. The elder Mr. Alam sat quietly and sipped his coffee as his eldest son, Zinnah, put his cup down.

"I have heard a lot of good things about you, Mr. Nizam Ahmed," said Zinnah. "I know you are the second most powerful man in the banking sector of our country."

Nizam smiled and waved his hand to gesture a change of subject. But Zinnah showed no interest. He persistently continued praising Nizam for his honesty and hard work—the qualities he said he generally would not attribute to men who held such power.

"I know some bank officials who can create fake documents for you and steal money from the bank, or sanction loans to people with bad credit," Zinnah said.

"Is that so?" Nizam felt forced to ask.

"Yes, and I can name at least ten of your friends who are doing that! They've stolen huge chunks of money from the government and relocated to America or Malaysia, or somewhere else."

"The country is full of such corrupt people," Nizam concluded.

"If it were not for people like you, Mr. Ahmed, Bangladesh would surely have gone down the drains by now!"

Zinnah then mentioned his success in the garment industry. He was a sub-contractor for a big American company and was a man of big ideas. In a loud, excited voice, he shared some of his business plans with Nizam and asked for his valued opinion.

"Have you been to the fish market lately?" Zinnah asked.

"Have you noticed any good fish there? Do you know where all our Hilsa and Rohu and Boal fish are going? America and England and Australia! Bangladeshi people basically float all over the world like gams of sharks, hounding for Bangladeshi fish."

Nizam smiled in response.

"It's a booming business and all I need is just half a million U.S. dollars."

This time, Nizam did not smile. He kept his eyes fixed on Zinnah, waiting for his next flow of promising ideas.

But Zinnah was suddenly out of words. He coughed intermittently and sipped his cold coffee. The elder Mr. Alam finally yawned and reminded everyone that it was time for his evening prayer. The prospective groom asked Shila for another cup of coffee. Nizam felt an urge to smoke.

"I know my father has reservations, about your daughter," Zinnah finally said, breaking his silence. "You see, by family tradition, all the daughters-in-law in our family are white like talcum powder. It's a must if you want to propagate good-looking offspring. But your daughter's complexion can be ignored. After all, she is the daughter of a man with power to sanction bank loans." Zinnah tried to smile.

Nizam excused himself from the room and went to consult Aandhi.

"Are you out of your mind?" Aandhi exploded. "What will happen to us if you lose your job? I have one more daughter to marry off and two sons to educate. How can you think of taking such a risk for that conniving man?"

"What else is there for me to do?" Nizam asked desperately. "This has been, what? The sixth proposal that is about to go away this year, isn't it? What do you think people will say about Shila tomorrow? How do you think she'll feel if she's rejected one more time for no fault of hers?"

"Ma, I don't want to marry now," Shila said in a soft voice. "Baba, I want to get my master's degree. I don't want to get married. I don't need to! I can get a job and take care of myself."

No one paid attention to Shila. She stood there unnoticed—sobbing and murmuring her big ideas about her own future—until Kheya heard her. Kheya stood by her sister and held her tightly in an embrace. "Don't cry, Shila," Kheya whispered. "It's not your fault that all these men are cruel and greedy and blind. I don't need the sun or the moon or the stars to tell me how pretty you are."

Shila smiled. "It's all right. I've grown used to it—being invisible to the mortal eyes, I mean," she said teasingly. "It gives me some sort of Godly strength."

Kheya did not say anything. Together, the two sisters stood quietly by the window, watching a dark sky that had absorbed all the futile twinkles of all the illumined stars, because light did not matter.

Nizam went outside to light a cigarette. He took a few long puffs and sent a bunch of smoke rings toward the sky. He then flicked his cigarette into the air and watched as it flew up like a firefly and came down like a shooting star. Nizam stomped on the fallen cigarette and went inside to see off his guests.

"Next Friday seems to be a good day for them to tie the knot," Nizam told Zinnah. "I have decided to throw a grand wedding party for my daughter and your brother. What do you say?"

WHEN OUR FATHERS DIE

I.

Dear Dr. S.,

Family tragedy hit me this weekend: my father died.

Sincerely,

Daniel Harrington

White letters labeled on the black cubes—85 cubes in total. Cubes that held secret keys to unlock the doors for unlimited words to rush in, like a ceaseless flood. But I sat motionless and let letters cluster and foam and fluff over my thoughts, like the caramel frothed topping that sits defiantly over my morning macchiato denying my lips their rightful access to the warmth of the nicely brewed coffee hiding underneath. Tilt the cup and it will spill. Keep it straight and your nose is frothed. You need to make a mess to avoid making one. Daniel didn't seem to be a fan of frothed topping. His was just direct brew. Dark Roast. Or blond, maybe. White man's coffee. How simply he could put a few letters together and hit "send." And his message was sent. Like his usual, a quite direct and simple approach.

"Are you from India, Dr. S.? No? Where is Bangladesh? But I don't get it…. why don't your people focus more on, what's it called? *Bingali* literature?"

"Let's focus here, Daniel. So what was I saying?"

"You were saying a text is an ontological being, a living, breathing specimen, just like one of those talking books in *Harry Potter*. How can a text mean anything if a reader has no freedom?"

"Wait 'til I get to the part where I will tell you about the death of an author."

"If the author is dead and the reader is powerless… Goodness, Dr. S., then what is the point of reading?"

"Nothing, Daniel. The point of everything is nothing, and beyond."

"This Barthes guy makes no sense to me!"

Daniel always had something to say, something to refute, or something to explain. Words would come to him easily and effortlessly, of course, because the Irish stiffness of his ancestral tongue was long dead and buried. He laughed every time I struggled on a word that didn't want to come out of my forked

tongue: one part third world, one part hyphenated American. My words were Rapunzel's exotic hair, frantically guarded by the mother not my own. Accidents were bound to happen if I did let that hair down. Words crawled and crept and slimed and slithered. Words got stabbed by the forked ends and caved in underneath my divergent tongue. If words were delicate foods cooked with sounds and winds, then I could have bragged of my culinary mastery at any great 'wordstaurant.' But words were nothing but vibration of the wind, plucking strings of the pinnate leaves of thoughts, filtering sound through tongue, lips, and jaw. And sometimes the wind would show its true color and try to topple a tree, with its roots hanging up and its pinnate leaves uselessly hanging down, like Rapunzel's chopped hair.

I was teaching Roland Barthes that day. And in my attempt to emphasize the slash that he had placed between a B and a P, I almost slashed out my calm.

"In the sixty-four lexicons of S/Z, Balzac," I started my lecture. And here came the faltering moment as I tried in vain to throw Balzac's 'Bal' as a ball and let the 'zac' fly away like a 'duck.' In my mouth, poor Balzac got trapped in the two vowel sounds in 'ballduck,' a word yet to be created by a non-

gentlemen said (and this time I didn't dare pronounce their names again): b is not p, s is not z. And I am not you."

On my way to the next class, I heard him telling someone, "Wait until you hear her say the words Balzac and Barthes. She sounds so funny."

In my next class, I talked about Barthes without mentioning Balzac.

After the Balzac episode, I became extra cautious to prevent accent mishaps. I would talk about "Minute On Education" but write down Macaulay's name on board. Macaulay was my other enemy.

"This guy," I would point at Macaulay's name written on the board, "is my Prospero, in a historical sense. My ancestors were all happy Calibans before he came. He brought his wand of knowledge and some of my ancestors became Ariels, while some learned how to curse their master."

I moved my dry erase wand over the board and my words turned into this relentless stream where Said and Fanon and Lacan floated without faltering. And every time I uttered a word unfriendly to my culturally relaxed facial muscles, I'd cast a secret glance at Daniel's face. A serious expression on his face would tell me my accent was not sharp enough to disrupt his attention. One smirk, one slight twitch of his lips, and I knew he got me. For a whole semester I was secretly haunted by a pair of ears that had the power to separate an echo from a sound. A shadow has a form to mimic, but echo is this shapeless, endless stir in the air that makes us aware of a vacuum, a caving emptiness. For me, Daniel Harrington was the caution sign of my void. My emptiness.

"You know Dr. S., my dad loves snakes."

"Okay."

"No, seriously. He has two big pythons. Very big. And a boa. He got them for free from his job."

"What do they eat?"

"Fresh meat, live rats—a bunch of them—and other living stuff. One of his snakes ate my Chihuahua once."

"Who feeds them, your mom?"

"Nah, Mom left him, 'coz the boa tried to eat her up one day and she asked my dad to choose between the snakes and my mom, and he chose his snakes." Daniel paused for a moment and then muttered in an almost inaudible voice: "she died last year, my mom. She had long wavy hair, you know, just like you."

"Black?" I asked curiously.

"No, red," he said. "But you resemble her in so many ways!"

I suddenly felt awkward, and did not know how to respond to the emotions of a grieving son who was seeing in me the reflection of his Irish–American mother. I redirected the conversation back to his living father.

"You live with your dad?" I asked.

"With my grandpa. When I was young, he always said that he might feed me to his snakes if I didn't do my homework, and that scared the hell out of me."

Daniel's father was snake-charmed. He was in love with Florida pythons. He lived on his airboat and worked as a ranger at the Everglades, the python capital of the world. If you saw a big python blocking your driveway or basking in your garden in Port Everglades, the first number that you called would be Daniel's dad's, and he would come with a big sack and tongs and hooks. One day, this little boy was playing with his dog in the backyard and came to find a nice brown stick. Who doesn't know dogs would be crazy-happy to have a nice stick to play with? The boy wanted to pick up the stick and throw it to his dog, a midsized cocker spaniel. But the stick that he picked up snapped and swirled in an attempt to coil around the little boy, and before the boy saw it, the dog saw it, and before the boy snatched his cocker away, the snake snatched it as the brave spaniel ran toward the coiling stick and barked its heart out until the Boa coiled around its soft, fluffy body, crushing and squeezing and rolling it close to the big mouth that swallowed the savior, head first.

Daniel's dad had already arrived at the place when the rolling process was halfway done, but he stood there as the Boa swallowed its prey. The homeowner came out with his shotgun but the ranger stopped him. It would be a sin to deprive a hungry creature of its meal, he told the others, and waited like an angel, guarding God's dangerous creature from other's venom. That was the boa that he later took as a pet: the same boa that ate Daniel's chihuahua and chose Daniel's mother as its next target.

Daniel Harrington, my accent nemesis, always waited outside my office, as if my office were the place where I had to go to listen to his stories. Stories about a father who loved snakes. About a mother who cooked whole grain rice with cannabis leaves as a special herbal remedy for her terminally ill friends. About his sister who was working at a strip club to pay for nursing school. And about Daniel, who wanted to be a college professor and teach literature, just like me. After his regular office visits, he walked beside me, like an oblique shadow, and accompanied me to a class, where he waited with his tongs and hooks to capture the hissing words that fell from the womb of my forked tongue.

My shadow left me for a week and reappeared as an email. *Family tragedy hit me this weekend: my father died.* A simple statement generated a flow of questions: how old was his father? What did he die of? Did he have the same blue eyes, Irish-red hair? Did he really intend to feed Daniel to his snakes? Was it his boa that took his life? Was it his heart that gave away the fight? Was Daniel standing by the hospital bed, watching his father turn into a memory as the cardio-hills on the screen started flowing like one horizontal line from one end of the screen to the other, in an attempt to reach the endless end of infinity? Did he watch his father's last breath mist on the disposable oxygen mask—the last mark of life— soon to be dumped in the hospital's trashcan? Did that last mist of life create any shape, any last message for the grief-stricken faces that crowded around the bed in a futile attempt to block death's way? What shape did my father's mist create on the oxygen mask that was strapped over his face, as if to suction death out of him, or thrust some life force in? Did he quiver a little when Dr. Yeng unplugged his life support? Did my father feel in his heart, somewhere in his blood-clotted, dead brain, that it was I—his precious daughter—who had given the signal to pull the plug?

He died alone, my father, in a hospital that was far away from his home. His wife stayed in the background, with four minor children, waiting and wishing for a miraculous cure that could save her husband, while the oldest child fancied herself a maestro abroad, pulling cords to end a life's opus or tapping keyboards to create a tantalizing dissertation on some transatlantic texts. A call from a distant hospital woke her up one winter night and asked her to make a decision about the fate of her comatose father. There were too many decisions for her to make in two weeks. She had to put an end to too many things. Fall semester had to end and a dissertation had to be submitted. A C-section date had to be confirmed; a bunch of trips had to be made to Babies 'R' Us, and a suitable departure time had to be decided in order to put an end to the piles of hospital bills accumulating over the suspended life of a brain-dead man.

in Singapore. Daniel's father's snakes were now the county's property. Daniel could get a new chihuahua and could easily move back home, once the snakes were sent back to the everglades of memories. This was not the case for me. My father's coffin was broken. My shadow grew taller every day and ate me up and spewed me out a thousand times. Every night it pulled me out of my bed and placed me before a mirror that only reflected the face of an executioner. And in my dreams, I was always Daniel's father's python that wrapped its weight around my own cracking conscience. Grief fades, but guilt does not.

The eighty-five tiny black cubes on my keyboard started tap dancing as I slowly began connecting letters, punctuations, and spaces to speak in a silent voice that surpassed all ethnic accents to console a grieving child whose eager ears could stay alert for a thousand years like an ageless deer, only to have a chance to chase the echo of a father's affectionate voice down through the rectilinear tunnel of time.

'Dear Daniel,' I started typing, 'I am so sorry to hear about your loss.'

And I sat there, not knowing what to type next.

THE
HYACINTH BOY

1: The Promise

"**I** am running away next month," Shojol said in a casual tone, keeping his eyes fixed on his rod floater wobbling in the water.

His three companions looked at him for a second and then decided to pay attention to the water beneath the bridge. The four of them had been meeting up on that bridge since grade school. Some days they brought their fishing rods, and some days they just sat there and chatted on things of no importance. Rodela was fourteen, and being the smartest one among them, she was considered the dumbest. Rana and Tito—being a year senior and being boys—considered themselves Rodela's guardians. It was Shojol who always saved Rodela from their uninviting guardianship. Shojol was seventeen, the oldest among them, and therefore the oddest.

Rodela shook her legs and swayed her hands in the air in an effort to keep the buzzing mosquitoes away. Tito suddenly became irritated at Rodela and chided her.

"Shhh, can you sit still at least once in your lifetime?" he hissed.

"I'm trying, I'm trying!" Rodela said peevishly, "but these bites—they itch!!"

"I think I caught something!" Rana gave a shout and jumped on his feet. But his excitement faded the moment he saw the big chunk of the water hyacinth plants entangled in his fishing hook.

"This is what happens when you let a talkative girl tag along with you everywhere," Rana said. "Girls are nothing but problems!"

"I've made up my mind." Shojol continued his

conversation, ignoring the commotion around him. "By the 7th of next month, I'm out of here. I'm leaving by train. I'll go find my dad and stay with him. I hate living here like this—" he abruptly stopped talking and looked away in the direction of the horizon beyond the waterline.

No one said anything. The four of them sat like a school of dead fish on the corner of a mutilated bridge over a dying lake swarmed with the invasive water hyacinth plants that spread their roots like endless spider veins through the legs of withered waters.

"Let's go home," Rana finally said. "We're out of luck today."

"You are always out of luck," Rodela said.

"I could have caught a huge fish today, if you didn't throw such a tantrum like a — like a cranky whale!" Rana replied. "I'll catch a ginormous fish someday—I promise you. I'll catch the biggest fish that one could ever find in this lake. I promise."

"We shouldn't bring girls to fishing," said Tito. "Next time, only three of us will come for fishing. Okay, Shojol?"

Shojol looked at his friends and began talking again. "I want to catch the morning train from Dhaka to Dinajpur—to the northernmost point of the country. From there, I'll jump the border to Patna, India. I'll take a train to Amritsar, and from there I'll go to Pakistan and then Iran. I'll ride camels to reach the Arab Sea and take a boat to Kuwait."

"Don't you need money, passport, and visa to hop borders like that?" Rana asked.

"Money, a little, but passport? No. I won't be traveling like you guys. I will smuggle myself—like some shipments of perishable goods. I'll blend in easily, with perishable goods, I mean."

"Isn't that dangerous?" Tito asked.

"I'll think about danger when it comes," Shojol answered. "For now, all I know is that I have to run away."

"But why?" Rodela asked. "Wouldn't your mother worry about you? Wouldn't you miss us?"

Shojol smiled at her as he continued. "Rahimuddin Uncle said my dad works for a cruise ship that sails through the Arab Sea. I am sure it won't be hard to track him down.

"But how'd you know him? Didn't he leave you and your siblings when you were mere toddlers?" Rodela sounded worried.

"He has the same birthmark that I have—this one right below my chin." Shojol showed them the mark.

"The same black bird shape! How cool!" Rodela said. "You will stop every sailing boat and yell, 'O sailors of the sea, show me your black bird sign and claim me as your son! Nice!"

Shojol smiled again.

"Can we come with you?" she asked.

"No."

"Can we see you off at least?"

"I'll meet you here in the morning," he said, "and you can walk with me halfway to the train station. But make sure to keep it a secret."

Shojol then took his leave. He had to go to Rahimuddin Uncle's store to pick up some groceries. His three friends sat there, feeling happy. Shojol was finally going to find some peace in life.

2: The Haunting

Shojol walked as fast as he could to reach home before dark. But the moment he remembered he had to stop at Rahimuddin Uncle's store on the way, his speed automatically slowed. Rahimuddin was a well-liked man, but Shojol was afraid of him. At seventeen, Shojol's voice was soft, and his face was smooth as coconut butter. With a headful of curly hair and a tall, slender body, he always stood noticeable in a crowd. But Shojol did not like to be noticed, especially by people like Rahimuddin. He carried in his head a list of men whom he considered dangerous. Rahimuddin ranked third on that list. Kana Bokul came second, and Milton's name came at the top.

Rahimuddin had become a self-appointed guardian of their family since the day he brought them a letter from Shojol's missing father. Shojol's mother instantly accepted him as a channel of hope and asked her three children to do the same. Shojol was only ten when that letter arrived, and he had been afraid of Rahimuddin ever since. His two siblings, on the other hand, had no problem accepting Rahimuddin's guardianship. They felt grateful to the man who brought them gifts and made their mother cook hearty meals for the whole family. They waited eagerly for Rahimuddin's regular Friday visits. On that day, Rahimuddin sent bags full of groceries, along with a preferred menu, which their mother had to follow—word for word. Rahimuddin came in the evening and ate dinner with the kids. After dinner, he always sat with them, telling them stories about their missing father—the man who jumped on a southbound ship to bring home loads of fortune from the Mediterranean lands. Because those stories lingered till midnight, Rahimuddin had to spend the night at their house. Even though his siblings loved it when Rahimuddin visted the house or sent them gifts, or stayed overnight, Shojol remained worried. He stayed anxious and watchful—of his mother, whose face looked pale when

like a pair of defiant suns, and his docile manhood rested—on a cushiony scrotum over a hidden cave of creation.

Kana Bokul's dead eye went numb and the living one closed itself instantly. He could not believe what he saw— standing in front of him—a human body that was more than one. His knees shook and his hands trembled. Unable to control his knees, Kana Bokul sat down on the dirty street and leaned on the wall. He closed his eyes and opened and closed them again—as if in an attempt to process the whole truth. All the while, Shojol stayed quiet and unaffected by Kana Bokul's reaction. He got dressed and said in a calm voice, "I have to go now." Kana Bokul slowly got back to his feet and placed his hand on Shojol's shoulder. He spoke in a surrendering voice, apologizing for his action.

"I had to see to be sure," he said, "and now that I've seen, I know what I have to do—for your safety. My God! You have no idea what grave danger you are in! Do you know what Milton and his gang are up to? They're planning to kidnap you and sell you to that pimp Matuli Hijra. And Matuli, I'm sure, will show you no mercy. But don't worry, I'll be your protector from now on."

"I don't need your protection," Shojol said calmly. "I can take care of myself. Besides, I'm not going to stay in this fucking town forever. I don't care about Milton, or that pimp, or you. In two weeks, I'll be gone."

"Where?"

"I won't tell you."

"Fine. But don't tell your plan to that bastard uncle of yours or to Milton, or anyone else. They'll kill you if they know you're planning to leave. And I won't tell anyone. And I will give you protection."

"I don't need to tell nobody nothing," Shojol snapped. "And I can take care of myself! I don't need a bodyguard."

Shojol walked away. Kana Bokul stood under the flickering lamppost by the street—wrapped in his own quivering shadow and lost in an enticing world of gain. What he saw tonight must be protected and should be invested. He had to see Matuli Hijra before it was too late. Kana Bokul started running.

With lips painted in red and eyes blotched in black and chest perked with padded bras and a stout body covered in a red sari, the magnificent Matuli Hijra came out to meet Kana Bokul.

"I found a package." Kana Bokul said breathlessly.

"What kind?" Matuli Hijra seemed disinterested.

"Multi."

"Is it the same package that Milton promised me?"

"I don't know what Milton promised you. But I know what I am going to bring. And I promise you haven't seen anything like that yet."

"I'll pay forty grand to whomever brings me a package that equipped."

"Then get your money ready," Kana Bokul said. "You'll get your package by the end of the week."

Kana Bokul left Matuli Hijra's house in haste. He had to close the deal before the prospect vanished in two weeks.

5: The Futility

The three friends arrived at their usual meeting place on the day Shojol was scheduled to leave the town. But Shojol did not show up. Not that day, or the next day, or the week after. Every day, long before sunrise and on their way back from school, the three of them waited for a friend who had promised to meet them one last time.

"To think of him as a good friend! How stupid we were!" Rana said one day. They were sitting on their bridge, with their fishing lines dunked in the shallow water.

"I never considered him good at anything," Tito said. "A seventeen year old boy and still in 9th grade with us! Come on."

"He was a good fisherman, though," Rodela said. "He could catch fish the way a fruit catches all the flies!"

"Yeah. A rotted fruit that he was. A rotten, bad friend," Tito said in an agitated voice.

Rodela tried to protest, but Rana gestured for her to keep quiet. He was about to catch a fish, he said, keeping his eyes fixed on the rod.

It was a crisp autumn evening. The western sky was lit with the last rays of the setting sun. The lake was covered with green and violet patches of water hyacinth. Violet flower clusters drifted over the green floating leaves like bands of autumn clouds in a calm sky. Each violet petal had a deep purple and blue shade with a yellow spark in the middle that looked like an eye. And the flower spikes with their bluish-yellow eyes floated like floral ommatidia—staring unblinkingly at the sky and into the water—as if it were their duty to guard some abysmal secret lying hidden under the shallow water. Rana's fishing pole suddenly gave a strong tug. The fishing rod was arched like a waning moon—sunken in the lake—and it tried to pull Rana down toward the water. The fish was too heavy for the rod and too sluggish to break away. Rana held the rod with his two hands while Tito took control of the spinning reel. Rodela held Rana from behind with her utmost strength. Together, they slowly walked from left to right, right to left, gradually pulling the fish toward the edge of the lake. They screamed and jumped and laughed in anticipation of a fish, which might be bigger than a whale. A big crowd formed around them. They clapped and cheered and waited with excitement. Then a group of people waded into the shallow water and began pulling the nylon line toward the land, slowly and carefully, until the fish came within range. They grabbed the big fish and pulled it toward the muddy shore.

It was huge, weighing more than a hundred pounds. Its dark eyes were blank, with swollen splotches of blood in the middle; its curly hair, darker than night, floated like the leaves of water hyacinth. Netted aquatic roots covered its face, like a protective veil. Violet spikes of water hyacinth flowers floated like floral corset over its once-plump breasts. The fish had legs instead of a scaly fin; its crotch was slit open, and strings of ovate hyacinth leaves hung loosely over its unfilled scrotum, trying to hide the gaping void of a deferred manhood from the relentless gaze of humankind.

MOTHER
IMMIGRANT

I

"*Habla español?*"

"No, sorry," Molly said apologetically.

"Your mother? Does she speak English?" This time the inquisitive lady pointed at the old woman, sitting beside Molly and joyfully waving at people.

"Not much," said Molly.

"She does, she does!" Molly's mother-in-law approached the old lady. "I, Noor Jahan," she said in a shy voice, "and you?" The old lady was equally receptive. "Esperanza," she introduced herself and stretched her hand expecting a handshake. But Noor Jahan gave her a hug instead and gestured her to follow her to the bench. The two elderly women then sat on the park bench and started chatting, using a mixed language of broken English, unceasing hand gestures, and unbound excitement. Seeing her mother-in-law comfortably settled, Molly went for her usual run, knowing, by the time she came back from her run, her mother-in-law might end up making friends with half of the people in the park. It was their daily routine. Every day after work, Molly brought her mother-in-law to the park for a walk. But Noor Jahan preferred sitting on a bench and chatting with people. Occasionally, she walked a few yards until she reached the next bench—her next chatting spot.

Noor Jahan collected stories from the park bench and spilled them out on their way back home like a bursting bag of popcorn. She loved to give nonstop lectures on the benefits of evening walks.

"Walking is a good exercise," she said. "I was telling Esperanza that if you can walk everyday for two miles, you can walk past every disease and live 100 years!"

"Who is Esperanza?" Molly could not help asking.

"Manuela's mom—the lady who approached you today, remember? By the way, why don't you walk with Manuela? She is a very good daughter, this Manuela. Almost your age. It'd be so good to see you with a friend!"

"I have friends!" Molly exclaimed.

"Nah. Those aren't your real friends—I don't think so." Noor Jahan said. Then without waiting for Molly's response, she started unfolding the trajectories of Esperanza's life. Of her six children, only Manuela stayed in Florida; the rest was scattered all over the country. Esperanza moved in with Manuela after her husband's death. Manuela was divorced, and her only son, a soldier, was stationed in Iraq.

"And you learned all these in one hour?" Molly asked. "You understood every word in English—and Spanish, too?"

"Language is never difficult, but people are." Noor Jahan said. "You have to train yourself to read the expressions and emotions of what you hear."

Being a highly opinionated woman, Noor Jahan always shared her views on every aspect of everyone's life. She had lived in Florida ever since she moved to the States with her husband and children forty years prior. She never went to school and could hardly communicate in English. But that never stopped her from expressing herself or imposing her views. She took pride in calling herself an American. "I am a daughter of two mothers," she always told her listeners. "One is my real motherland, and the other is the motherland I adopted. Because my children love the immigrant motherland more, I have learned to love her. I, too, am American now."

After her husband passed away, Noor Jahan's children sold her house and helped her downsize. They then took turns in taking care of her. They wanted her to divide her time among the ten of them. But after a few years of hopping from one house to another, Noor Jahan refused to abide by their rules. She expressed her desire to live with Jamal and Molly, because she considered Molly the best cook among all her daughters-in-law. At first, her older sons objected to the idea, but they all eventually surrendered to the obstinacy of their mother. "I'm not your luggage, so stop trying to carry me around," she had told them.

She had been living with Molly since then. Even though they were very attached to their grandmother, Molly's three children sometimes found her nonstop chattering a bit distracting, especially in the afternoon when they sat to finish their schoolwork. To resolve that issue, Molly started bringing her out for a walk in the park. Her children and her husband enjoyed two hours of peace and quiet every afternoon while Molly kept herself busy—driving Noor Jahan around the town, taking her to the park, and listening to the endless rant of the enthused woman who firmly believed that the world might go awry if she went silent.

"Dilruba's mother could not believe I am turning seventy-five this year. 'Apa, you don't look a day older than fifty,' she told me the other day." She reported to Molly, as they were driving back from the park. "I told her, all it takes is the two-mile walk that I take with Molly every day and the healthy food that Molly feeds me. Poor woman, she suffers from constipation, and do you know Dilruba does not buy for her the pitted prunes because they consider them expensive? She gets her the cheaper brand. I told her I would ask you to buy the kind that you get for me. Will you...?"

Molly promised to buy a pack of pitted prunes for Dilruba's mother. Molly's friend Dilruba was not a fan of Noor Jahan's babbling mouth. But Dilruba's mother considered Noor Jahan the wisest woman in the community as did all the other elderly women of every Bangladeshi household. Noor Jahan was their mirror where they saw the reflections of their past glories and present gloom. These elderly women waited eagerly for months, expecting to be invited to a social gathering where they could sit around Noor Jahan and listen to her endless tales. For these immigrant mothers, Noor Jahan came as a messenger from their past. The hosts generally considered her a disruptor in such gatherings. Noor Jahan's presence in a party would mean a shift of attention—from the center to the margin: the glamorous new world of the hostess looked dull and lay dead, under the ashes of a world of memories. The hostesses of such parties sometimes tried to exclude Noor Jahan from their guest lists. But the plot always failed because of the interventions from their mothers.

"Don't bring your mother-in-law this time, "Dilruba told Molly when she invited her to a potluck at her house.

"But your mother has already invited her!" Moly said. "She is really looking forward to being there. And I can't leave her home with the kids. She feels lonely and neglected, you know. The kids stay busy with their lives and don't spend much time with her. So, she is coming with me."

At the party, Noor Jahan made herself comfortable in the living room amidst the invited guests and took control of every conversation string like a master puppeteer.

"Auntie, you want to watch a new Bangla movie after dinner?" Dilruba tried to break Noor Jahan's spirit. "Don't you want to try my lobster curry? I cooked it following your recipe."

"Yes, yes, I will, but let me finish my story first," said the spirited lady. "Molly, can you warm up the lobster curry for me? As I was saying, my husband knew how to do his grocery. If he bought Hilsa fish, he would buy eggplants. No, not the round kind, the long ones. And for Koi fish, he would buy cauliflower and peas. What, Rohu fish? He liked it cooked with potatoes and green tomatoes. He always liked the fish head cooked with mung beans. You don't know how to cook fish head? Very easy! Sauté the fish head with onion, turmeric, cumin, coriander, garlic paste—what, ginger? Nononono, we never use ginger with fish. Ginger goes only with meat, you see. My husband used to say—"

"Auntie, you want some dessert?" Dilruba asked.

"Yes, thank you. But listen to this first. I was very scared when I first came to America. Mr. Nixon was the President, or was it Reagan? One of them, but that's not the point. The point is I came here directly from a remote village in Bangladesh. I never visited Dhaka or any other place. I rode a plane before riding a train, hahaha. And when the plane landed, I saw snow, and I thought, *Subhanallah*, these people don't have to buy ice chunks from the bazaar during Ramadan! Allah must love this country very much. He gave this country ice directly from heaven to make lassi and fruit punch for *iftaar!* My husband said, 'Rajiv's Mother, take a look at the trees stacked in Nature's fridge,' and I said, 'I hope they saved their *paan* trees from this snow.' I had this habit of chewing paan from a very young age, and—"

The story continued until Jamal intervened.

"Mother, let's go," he said, and Noor Jahan instantly lost the thread of her story basket, only to reclaim it on their way home. "Dilruba is such a nice woman, and she cooks so well. Jamal, have you tried her lobster curry? She mixed the exact ingredients to give it the desired taste and flavor. Your father would have loved this dish. Listen to this, Molly. During our youthful days, your father-in-law and I…"

Molly had heard the story so many times that even if the old woman stopped narrating at this point, Molly could still see her unspoken words, waiting like a band of excited bulls to pierce through their matador's vocal capote. Molly closed her eyes to dodge them.

Molly was always intrigued by the old woman's extraordinary power to mute silence. For this woman, every word was an illimitable allusion. If someone threw her a word, she would reimburse with a thousand new ones—not crumpled or burnt or clumped but crisp, fresh words, dipped in memories and images of more words to come. She'd put bead after bead on a long string of sound, place a hoop here and a loop there, until the world of bygone days—with all its sounds and shapes and smells and colors—dangled with utmost poise at the tip of her tongue like dewdrops beaded on the strings of sun-dipped grass.

Insomnia kept Noor Jahan awake, sometimes all night. Every night, she took a bath or drank a cup of warm milk and waited eagerly in her bed to catch a few glimpses of sleep. Then she got up and walked around the house for an hour or two before finally tapping on Molly's door: "Are you sleeping? Molly?" She tapped and scratched like a desperate dog until Molly came out. "Come to my room. I have a new story to tell you…" Molly would follow the old woman and drop flat on her bed like a broken pine log while the accidental Sheharzaad whispered away her stories in a series of endless epiphanies.

Noor Jahan's other children sometimes invaded her world, demanding her presence in their lives, and in the process, displacing her from home to home for a few months. But Noor Jahan never took her mirth and her story basket with her when she travelled. Her stories belonged in Jamal's house, with Molly and her three children, whom she considered her ideal listeners. "Ma should start spending more time with her other children, you know," Jamal said one day. "Afzal was saying that you are too bossy and you don't let them come close to her. He wants us to go back to the previous arrangement that we had. Twelve months equally divided among ten children—each of us will get six weeks of her time."

Molly frowned at the idea.

"What do you think?" he asked again. "At least she'll be able to socialize more that way. Besides, there are a good number of Bangladeshi families in Miami, Atlanta, Savannah . . . " Jamal kept counting the places Noor Jahan would be visiting .

"Yes. But they are all scared of your mother."

"Why? Is my mother a ghost?"

"Not that. She is not actually the social type, especially when she's out of her comfort zone."

"Then we should definitely agree with the rotation arrangement. It'll do her good."

In Miami, Afzal took extensive measures to make his mother comfortable at his house and arranged weekly social gatherings on a regular basis. Jamal visited her every other Sunday, and each time she saw him, Noor Jahan only asked, "Are you here to pick me up?" Then, finding no positive response from her son, she walked back to her room, closing the door behind her. But one day, during one such visit, Jamal found his mother waiting for him—all packed and ready to leave.

"I'm coming home with you," she said. "Afzal's wife is a lousy cook and I can't sleep if I change beds."

With Noor Jahan's return, Molly's silent house regained its cacophonic rhythm.

II.

Noor Jahan made sure to remind all her daughters-in-law that she was the reason. She was the center, the Alpha woman. Afzal's wife, Jhumu, resented the way the old woman tried to rub her face in it.

"I can't stand her constant bragging!" Jhumu blurted out one day. "The whole time she was staying with us, all she did

was brag. 'You've come this far in life because of my doctor
son,' she kept telling me on and on. The old broken record!
What, as if I couldn't have found a better husband than Afzal,
she thinks? Should I tell her the only thing her doctor son is
good at is shoving his fingers in his patient's ass and sticking in
pipes and tubes to clean their shit? Making money by looking
at assholes and shit from seven in the morning? Sometimes
he grosses me out so much that I cringe in disgust when he
touches me. What if his gloves tore off when he was poking
someone's colon, and what if he forgot to wash his hands
afterwards? God knows what shit is sitting in his fingernails—
yellow shit, white shit, black shit, Bangla shit, Hindu shit,
Muslim shit — I don't give a shit as long as you clean up
properly, man! Just don't stick it in me if you are covered in
other people's shit! And then there is this foulmouthed woman
of a mother-in-law, always poking with her sharp words. I
don't know how you handle her."

Molly could hear the old woman weaving her usual
basket of stories for her daughters in the next room:

"My only brother came to this country after the English
sahibs left India. When my brother sent us plane tickets, one
for your grandpa and one for me, your grandpa sold his house
to buy tickets for your three uncles and your dad. Nazma
didn't need a ticket because I tucked her inside my womb,"
she chuckled. "We packed our lives in five big suitcases and
jumped on board. But when we unpacked, you know what we
found? Two more daughters, a few more sons, and then along
came all these crawling ants!"

"We are not ants!" the girls protested.

"No, you are not ants. Squirrels; that's what you are;
little squirrels. Always munching on chips, or candies, always
running around."

"Mom! Granma is calling us squirrels!"

Molly never meddled in these short-lived fights. She knew the twins would always stick with the old woman, like a pair of wings on her back, ready to flutter through the lands of her never-ending tales.

"Granma, tell us how you got married," the twins asked her once.

"Your grandfather was a young man of twenty years. He was a student at Presidency College, in Kolkata, you know. He used to come visit his grandparents in Khulna every summer. One morning, I was trying to climb a guava tree to get some ripe guavas. A young man was fishing in the bend of the Madhumoti River that swerved by our house. The moment I saw him, I jumped off from the tree and tried to run. But he came forward and climbed the tree to get some guavas for me. After that day, he would pick some perfectly ripe guavas and wait for me by the river. I'd sit by him and watch him fish. I ate at least a hundred guavas in seven days that summer! Before he went back to Kolkata, the man came to visit my parents, and we were married the next year."

"How old were you?"

"Let me think. India just became a free country, and I was born twelve years before that—yes, so that would make me thirteen, or fourteen."

"How awful!" Did you do it that young?" One of the twins asked.

"Do what?"

"You know…"

"Wasn't that child-molesting? Uhm, I know! Pedophile, the word is pedophile," one said.

"Was grandpa a pedophile?" asked the other.

"What is this pedofedo thing you are talking about? Your grandpa was no such fedo. He liked me and proposed to my parents and married me, that's all!"

"How can you marry so young?" one said.

"Why did you get married if you didn't do that thing?" the other asked.

"Well, well! Now I see which curiosity is killing these two little mice here! No, we didn't do your THING until I was sixteen."

"Yew! Disgusting!" They screamed together. "We are almost thirteen now."

"Is that so? Then let's ask your dad to start looking for suitable grooms."

"Mom! Granma is talking nasty!"

"You call it nasty, and I call it a miracle! Think what would have happened if your grandpa didn't go visit his grandparents in Khulna, and I didn't have that craving for the guavas! I wouldn't have married him, and my brother would not have sent plane tickets for an unmarried sister to come to a foreign land! And you wouldn't be American if I wasn't here first, see?"

"But don't you miss your home?" the twins wanted to know.

"What home? Home is not where you are from. Home is where you live. Home is where your children and grandchildren are. Home is where you die. This is my home, because this is where I will die."

"But, Granma, don't you miss speaking to your friends back home—in your own language?"

"I'm speaking in my language with you, aren't I? I like the way you speak with me—in slurred and broken Bangla—so adorable! You see, language doesn't make or break people. People break people. When your spirit is intact, no language in the world can bar you from expressing your feelings," said Noor Jahan.

III.

There were times when the Bangladeshi community of West Palm Beach desperately sought Noor Jahan's company. They wanted her to entertain their lonely mothers with her endless stories of home and hope. Sometimes they paid uninvited visits, bringing with them mothers who they said were getting desperate to be around the town's most talkative Bangladeshi woman. At these gatherings, surrounded by her eager listeners, Noor Jahan unfolded shiny new stories from her sheath and mesmerized her audience with her words. She played the role of a powerful magician, letting each word clash and clang and clank and whoosh with the next word to create a desired impact. And as she spoke, a group of dislocated old arthritic bones sat around her, like broken stems of a tree with unsettled roots—clutching as strongly as they could to the fluid fizzles of memories that were being recounted by an elderly woman in the only language they knew. And sometimes, after she was done telling stories, she took the role of a caring sister, asking those lonely women to spend a few nights under her hospitality.

"Can you please make some fish curry tomorrow, for Shelley's mother?" she asked Molly once. "Shelley's husband is diabetic and makes everyone follow a strict diet in his house. Rahela has been living on roti and vegetables for months. Tell me, can a seventy-year-old Bangladeshi woman live without rice and fish curry?"

From her worried tone, Molly could sense the expected duration of her houseguests. Sometimes they stayed for a weekend, and sometimes for the whole week. And all the while, as Molly stayed busy preparing meals for her honored guests, her mother-in-law kept weaving tantalizing stories to entertain them.

"Don't use coriander seeds in the mutton curry. Seema's mother doesn't like coriander. Why are you smiling? What's so funny? Can't I know about someone's personal choices just because I haven't met her before today? Do you know what the problem is with your generation, Molly? You're preoccupied with your own stuff. Always *my kids, my husband, my job, my house*; there's no room for an other in your world. It's only I and mine!" The old woman had gone furious for no reason.

When she first came to live with Molly, the old woman was quite shocked to know that Molly and Jamal did not know much about their next-door neighbors. Jeanne was originally from France and her husband, Dustin, was from North Carolina, both software engineers, Molly had told her. They had two kids and three dogs. Molly didn't know where Jeanne grew up, or how she met Dustin. Molly didn't know what Jeanne's favorite French food was. The old woman became very concerned about Molly's social health. She could not figure out how two families lived so close for years and still treated each other like complete strangers.

"Only if I could speak English, I would have turned all these strangers into friends!"

It was Neal who took the task of an English teacher and made his grandmother sit with him and watch all his favorite shows. The old woman watched every cartoon with him for years, and yet she failed to learn the language. Eventually, she learned to understand the words spoken by the characters in Lifetime movies and stayed glued to the TV screen.

"Shhh, I can't talk now," she said before hanging up on one of her daughters one night. "The woman just found out that her husband has been sleeping with another woman. She is going to kill him and frame the mistress. She wants to buy a gun."

"How do you know? Do you understand what she said?" Molly asked.

The old woman didn't answer. She did not like to talk during her Lifetime channel hours. But she would happily spend the rest of her time giving advice to anyone she considered in dire need of her help.

"He is so skinny! This doctor! Maybe his wife doesn't let him eat enough rice," the old woman whispered, while the doctor stayed busy checking her blood pressure.

"The doctor is very handsome, and he is from Poland. They don't live on rice," Molly tried to explain.

"Nonsense! No one can live without rice. Tell him to eat rice once a day. Tell him, Molly, tell him!"

"Do you have a question or something? Noor Jahan, is there any problem?"

"My mother-in-law says you are a very good doctor."

"Thank you, Noor Jahan!"

Noor Jahan blushed as the doctor gave her a pleasant smile.

"Don't be so shy when people call you by your name," Molly had told her so many times. "It's your name. Why do you cower from it?"

"It sounds so strange! You see, no one calls me by my name anymore."

Her parents died decades ago. Her siblings called her "sister," and her husband called her "Rajiv's mom."

"Why did he call you that? You are my dad's mom too!" Neal once asked.

"Because it is the custom. The wife goes by her eldest child's name."

"What did he call you before Uncle Rajiv was born?"

"Nothing. He just made a hand gesture or shouted some gibberish to catch my attention."

"I don't get it," Neal said. "How'd you know he was talking to you? You'd always have to keep your eyes fixed on him to make sure, no?"

"You talk too much. Back in the days, kids did not dare ask so many questions. They were very respectful to their grandparents. I once asked my grandmother—"

"Mom! Granma's trying to tell me another story!" Neal screamed.

IV.

Noor Jahan was a roaming mother. To fulfill her obligation as the only living parent of her children, she had to visit them in different states. And every time she made these trips, she complained about her brittle bones and her aging spirit. And yet, despite her physical limitations, she had to go state-hopping in order to be with the children who demanded her company— sometimes out of affection, and sometimes out of need. But when her youngest son, Azmol, expressed his need to have his mother with him, the old woman vehemently objected.

"Molly, tell Azmol I can't go with him."

"Why doesn't she want to go? My kids need to spend time with her, just like yours!" Azmol said.

"She is standing right here. Why are you asking me?" Molly grunted.

"Don't let him take her, Mom," the twins whispered. "There are ghosts in Uncle Azmol's house. Granma is scared of ghosts."

"Is your wife on maternity leave still?" Molly wanted to know.

"Why do you bring Rini into this discussion?" Azmol snapped. "I just don't think it's good for Ma's health to stay in this hot weather year after year. She should stay with us in Savannah for a few months."

Noor Jahan reluctantly packed her bags and followed her youngest son, like an obedient daughter.

"Do you think we can stop this ridiculous living arrangement that you guys have made for her?" Molly asked her husband that night. "She is seventy-five years old. How does Azmol expect her to babysit his two youngsters and a newborn, eight hours a day?"

"Why are you so fussy about it? Let Azmol decide how long he wants to keep his mother with him. It shouldn't be your headache; she isn't *your* mother," Jamal said, as he turned off the light.

Jamal's agitated words kept Molly awake all night. Words. Sometimes they drizzle, drop by drop, like strings of pearls on a spear of grass. And sometimes they fall like shattered glass and pierce through open wounds.

V.

One year later, Azmol's wife, Rini, came to drop off the old woman. She blamed her for being clumsy and forgetful and called her an unfit grandmother.

"Can you believe she forgot to feed the baby one afternoon?" Rini sounded furious. "She always cried if we went out for a few hours or left her in the house even for a day! Do you know what she did last weekend? She ran away! Didn't even turn off the security alarm! We took the kids to Tybee Island for Thanksgiving weekend. All she had to do was warm up food and watch her Bangla TV, and she couldn't even do that! Saturday morning, the police called Azmol. The security alarm was buzzing nonstop and the front door was open. There was no sign of his mother in the house. We had to rush back home, and you know where the police eventually found her? Four blocks away, by Laurel Grove, an old cemetery where they used to bury the slaves centuries ago! She said she was helping a little girl find her mother. Can you believe it? And after that incident, she stopped talking to us. She kept badgering me to bring her back to you. She kept saying she wanted to go home. I mean, what is this? I am her daughter-in-law, too! Why does she consider your home as hers?"

After Rini left, Molly sat by her mother-in-law and softly asked, "What's wrong? What happened?"

"Nothing," the old woman said. "I want to go home."

"You are home, aren't you?" Molly wiped her tears as she hugged the old woman.

"No, " said the old woman calmly. "My real home. This country is not for old people like me."

"What do you mean? What happened in Savannah?"

But Noor Jahan said nothing. The Savannah trip had changed her. She seemed to have lost her enthusiasm for words.

After constant coaxing, Neal and his twin sisters finally succeeded in making her talk about the trip. The three siblings nestled around her one night, with their eyes fixed on her face. No word, not a single expression erupting from her mouth would escape them. In a sad, soft voice, Noor Jahan finally started narrating her story.

In Azmol's hundred-year-old house, even the oak trees in the backyard were older than her. Azmol and his family lived downstairs, while Noor Jahan lived upstairs in the only guest room of that house. In the morning, the wooden floor of her room always cracked and screeched, and at noon, the walls of her tiny room at the farthest end of the lonely corridor throbbed like a human heart: dipdip, dipdip, dipdip, dipdip, deep. And if she listened closely, she could hear a faint voice of a sickly child. At night, that faint voice became a prominent groan and then turned into a nonstop chant: "Help me! Mamma, help me. Mamma, help!" Noor Jahan always stood by the four walls of that room, stroking them with her two hands all night long, and crying with the voice of that little girl until sunlight peeped through the windows. She would fall asleep then—yes, that little girl, and Granma, too. But whenever Azmol, Rini, and the kids went away for weekends, she could hear the little girl's cry for help floating throughout the house all day long. "Help me, Mamma! Help!"

At night, when the hardwood floor of the lonely house squawked and the hanging moss from big oak trees lashed on the window panes and the little girl's cries for help turned into violent screams, Noor Jahan could not stay in her tiny room anymore. She ran to the porch outside and sat by the pool. One such night, when she was about to come out of her tiny room, a shadow suddenly melted through the walls and crawled over the floor and whirled into a shape of a girl, with long curly black hair and thin skeletal hands. The shadow with skeletal hands pulled the end of her sari and sobbed, "Help me, h-e-l-p-m—eeee—he—elp!"

"How can I help you, girl? What can I do?"

"I want to see my mamma. Take me home," the little girl sobbed and stretched her skeletal hand.

Noor Jahan held the girl's hand and ran out of the house, in search of a home without any direction. She did not remember how long she ran, or what made her go to that old graveyard. She only remembered that when they reached the cemetery, the little girl let her hand go and vanished.

"Where did she go, Granma? Why did she leave you?" they asked.

The old woman held her three grandchildren in a tight embrace. Then, after a while, she looked at Molly and said, "I want to go home, Molly. Will you take me there?"

VI.

The old woman did not want to walk with her from store to store in the mall. Molly found a nice bench by the food court, bought her an Auntie Annie's pretzel and lemonade, and warned her not to move an inch from the bench as she ran back to Macy's. She ran from kid's section to men's, from cosmetics to shoes, and from bedding section to kitchen section. In the meantime, the old woman finished her almond pretzel and managed to disappear among a drifting crowd.

Molly came back to find an empty bench, with a few almond crumbs and some crumpled napkins scattered around it. She could see the empty lemonade cup peeping through the trashcan nearby. She must have left in a hurry, Molly thought, looking at the litter. Molly ran from one corner of the mall to the other. She went to Auntie Annie's and asked if they had seen a big, tall, Indian woman in a white sari. She had always wanted to meet Auntie Annie and ask for the pretzel recipe, Molly told them. She ran to the information booth to request a missing person announcement. Finally, a mall security guard came to her rescue. He had seen an Indian woman outside the food court, by the restrooms.

In front of the men's restroom, a crowd stood, forming a human pretzel shape. Noor Jahan stood in the middle of that pretzel, wearing an expression of emptiness in her face. As Molly walked into the center, the empty face cracked a wrinkle of relief. The large cup of lemonade filled her up and she'd got to go. She knew Molly took her to one of these places with cartoon figures drawn on the door. In her anxious haste, she could not recall which sign was meant for her, and instead of entering through the door with a triangle topped with a circle, she entered the one that had no triangle on it. The Good Samaritan who had escorted her out of men's room introduced himself.

"What's wrong with her?" the gentleman wanted to know. "I asked her if she was lost. I even showed her the ladies' room. But she didn't say anything. She just gave me a blank look."

"What kind of a daughter are you, to leave an old woman all by herself like this?" someone accused.

"Why don't you buy her the disposable briefs if you have to bring her to the mall?" another asked.

"I am sorry for her misconduct, but let us pass through please!" Molly tried to walk away, holding tightly the anchal of a white sari that wrapped itself around Noor Jahan's rugged old body. But Noor Jahan refused to move.

"These foreigners," another said. "Why do they live in this country if they don't want to learn English?"

"Ma, please, let's go," Molly insisted.

"Is she a retard or something?"

"She doesn't speak much," Molly said, desperately trying to pull away the old woman's stone statue from the disarrayed center.

"I am sorry. I didn't realize she was mute." The Good Samaritan apologized.

"I didn't say she is. She just does not speak English."

"*NO. SHE DOES NOT!*" Noor Jahan suddenly screamed. "*She no foreigner, too! She from Bangladesh. But she American! She speaks Bangla, but she understands you. Do you UNDER-STAND HER? She asking you!*"

Noor Jahan clapped her hands and ground her teeth. She raised her right index finger upright, pointing at each and every one of the crowd as she spoke. Her mouth foamed and her eyes glared. Her feet fluttered as if they were standing on burning ground. The anchal of her sari fell from her shoulder and danced like a wind-struck sail. Amidst a slowly dissipating human pretzel, Molly stood motionless and watched the woman's rhizome voice grow and grow and grow—like a giant timber bamboo—in search of the last rays of a lost sun.

DARKLING,
I LISTEN

Darkling, I listen to the silence of a starry night and watch the boundless sky brooding over the silhouetted plants confined within the earthen pots in my rooftop garden. Standing by the darkened trees, I look down and watch the flow of energy running through the busy streets—like blood—through veins—till life resigns. I've been half in love with easeful death. For me winter comes, but spring never arrives. For me every month is the cruelest April—breeding neither lilac nor life. I fall upon the thorns, trying to bleed, but instead I drown in endless apathy: twenty-four hours a day and three hundred sixty-six days—in a leap year. For me each day is longer than a month; each month, longer than a year; and each year, longer than life. Days are slow. Nights—like life—run slower. Grandma used to say that life never ends for a woman. I didn't believe her then. But now that she's a ghost, I do. Life seems endless because I'm a woman. Or at least that's what I think they want me to be. They think I am a woman, because I look like one, so therefore, I must be—the whole baggage—a woe, not a man. I bleed every month like a woman; therefore, I must be one. I mean, I was—until the moment of truth hunted me down and pinned me on the wall, like a dried out beetle. Why did that moment have to come? Why can't truth for once be what we want it to be instead of being what it is? Why can't we create our truths the way we knit our lies? Why can't we make up prisms of our beautiful— dreamlike—fairytale—truths? What is truth, anyway? I have no Jesus to ask. I am my own Christ and my own cross. I nail myself to my cross and bleed misery. Still I don't die. Or, I rise from the dead to die again.

I shouldn't think crucifixion though. My faith requires me to ask for Almighty's forgiveness five times a day. But before that, I am required to ask for my husband's forgiveness. And before that, I have to make sure that I am forgiven by a whole lot of women—women who are my husband's mother, sisters, grandmothers, or aunts. God will forgive me, but my husband may not; my husband will forgive me once his mother does, which she will not. Religion-bound as she is, my mother-in-law believes a son's heaven is hidden beneath his mother's allegorical feet. And a good wife as I am supposed to be, I must seek my heaven under my husband's feet. But a good man as he is, he always keeps his wife's redemption on hold until he can secure his own place in heaven. Together, we form a divine queue— waiting to stick our heads under the feet of our designated paradise. Allah's forgiveness depends on his—not Allah's, my husband's—disposition. But a husband never forgives a woman of my kind. If my mother-in-law is right, then I am a foul-mouthed bitch that eats like a pig and yawns like a cow all day long and sleeps through the night like a buffalo. I am also a man-eating whore who moans like a cow all night long and soils a good husband's bed with unnecessary flow of fluid. I am wasting vital gametes by letting them slip through the dungeon of hell that lies between my legs. In other words, because I do not hold them in, I am not a woman.

Two hundred long ten years ago—when I was twenty—I met Amir at my cousin's wedding and got married within two weeks. Amir told me that his was the kind of love that happens at first sight. The moment he saw me, he thought I was the one. This idea of love sighting never made sense to me. Love is nothing but a fertile womb of cliché. One falls in it, gets blinded by it, loses sanity in the name of illogical emotional attachments, then sells one's soul or rather kills it to make room for the other. There are no two beings in love: there's only one—the one who is stronger, the one who absorbs the other like a sponge, eats the other like a flesh-eating bacteria. In order for love to be love, there has to be a murder. One soul dies so that the other rises like a shining sword, smeared in blood but labeled as loved. One sacrifices like a saint so that the other rises like one. In love, compromise is another name for euthanasia. I was never a sucker for such clichés of love. I believed in hatred at first sight, because in hatred, no one compromises. My mother-in-law hated me at first sight as if I were the femme fatal—lusting for the soul of her son. I hated her because she was the mother of the man whom I was forced to marry.

I was in love with Reza. Reza didn't care about leaving human specimens behind once he died. "Children are a nuisance," he used to tell me. "They eat up all our time and energy and money. I don't want you to get pregnant—EVER!" He always emphasized the last word so vehemently that I had to give him my assurance right away—before the word lost its weight. "Don't worry, I won't. NEVER!" I could say that with such confidence because I knew it to be true. My parents knew it too. But Reza didn't. He thought I was being generous, and I thought he was my chance. So I loved him. But that bastard married an immigrant visa-girl from his neighborhood and flew with her to New York. And with him flew away my fairy tale. Things that we revere the most generally come with wings. Birds. Dreams. Love. Hope. Money. Time. And in my case, a uterus.

When Reza was gone, my fertile mind was the only thing that helped me outlive the barren days. In most of my daydreams, I used to envision myself in New York. It always snowed in my dreams, the way it does in the movies, and I always walked through a snow-white Central Park. While walking like a distraught snow woman, I would suddenly hear somebody screaming my name "D—a—i—s—eee—yyyyyy!" I would freeze—the way heroines do in the movies—and slowly turn my head, with my long wavy hair lashing against my frostbitten face. I would see Reza running toward me in slow motion. Why is it that the climactic scenes in movies are generally run in the speed of a snail? Suspending a feeling of satisfaction or producing it in a slow-released medicinal dosage does not promise a prolonged desire. Like a shiny book cover of a romantic novel, it only offers, for a very brief moment, a flimsy fence between delusions and impending displeasures. I never allowed disappointments in my dreams, though. I let Reza hold me in a tight embrace and kiss me passionately, and I made him mutter nothing but poetry in my ears: "I've been roaming the roads of this earth for a thousand years. Much have I traveled, from the seas of Sinhala—through the dark nights—to the oceans of Malay.... And the one who brought me a moment's serenity was ...."

Tonight, standing in my rooftop garden and hearing long lost poetry inside my head, I imagine myself as a lighthouse, lighted.

Mothers are born with two uteruses. One keeps the fetus safe inside the womb, and the other tries to save her child from all possible adversaries of the world. My mother's second uterus was the fiercest. It never let the world come close to my secret. She exploded in anger when my father asked her to tell Amir the truth about me.

"What truth is there to tell?" she said. "My daughter is pretty and has a college degree in literature. And she'll make an excellent housewife. Where do you see a problem in that?"

"Tell them what you just told me," pleaded my helpless father. "They'll understand."

"There's no truth to tell. Besides, does every marriage need to bring children? What if Amir has infertility? Did you consider the idea of asking him for his health record?"

"But this is different. The doctors did what they had to do to save Daisy's life." My father sounded desperate.

"You just want me to tell them my daughter doesn't have a baby-carrying pouch inside her? If that's not such a big deal, why don't you do it?"

"I tell you they'll understand. Amir's mother seems to be a nice person. Being a mother of four daughters, she'll understand," my father persisted.

He was a hopeless dreamer, my father. For some strange reason, he thought women were real people. I wish I could have awoken him from his utopian dream. I wish I could have told him that in his country, a woman is a house that a man enters to leave behind his prints. And a woman without her pouch is like a door that opens to no house. I wish he had known that in his country, his daughter is not even a woman, let alone a real person.

And a Tiresias I am not. I did not experience the pleasures of being a woman until I was not one.

"She's an empty drum," my mother-in-law used to tell her relatives. "That Cambridge-educated father of hers has played us. How conveniently he forgot to mention that his daughter is nothing but an empty vessel! And the girl is more conniving than her cunning parents, I'm telling you! The moment she saw my son, she knew he was a good catch, and instantly spread her legs like a fishing net."

That woman and her jabbering mouth! She could run it nonstop like a sewing machine. Oh, how I always enjoyed shutting her off from my senses every time she started that machine of hers! I locked myself in my room and sat by the open window, closing my eyes, my ears, and every pore of my skin. I always eclipsed her voice—with my body thus locked and my mind distanced— and experienced the joyful birth of my quiescent silence.

When I was ten years old, the Queen of England heard of me. She paid attention to my name and acknowledged it with a smile. "I told Her Majesty about you," my father wrote in a postcard, "when our graduating class went to meet her at the palace. We all stood in line as the Queen walked by, shaking hands with each of us. She asked me about my family and I told her I have a very smart daughter named Daisy. And you know what she said? She said she was delighted to know of you!"

My father delivered his message in a beautiful postcard, which had a picture of Queen Elizabeth, smiling, over a magnificent palace by a tulip garden. After the postcard arrived, the queen followed me everywhere. At night, I stacked a pile of pillows on my bed and seated the postcard on it and stared directly at her bright eyes. "I'm proud to have made your acquaintance, Your Majesty!" I whispered to the postcard Queen who sat royally on the throne of pillows and smiled graciously at me until I fell asleep.

The smiling face of the queen flashed through my head this morning, when my father called.

"What have I done?" He sounded heartbroken. "How did I let that scoundrel marry you! How did I—"

"Don't cry, Papa," I said, smiling. "please don't blame Amir. He only agreed to remarry because his mother wants grandchildren. It's his duty to make his mother happy."

"It's all my fault! I should have known! But I won't let you stay in that house anymore! I'm coming for you tomorrow."

My father hung up before I could tell him that nothing could ever be his fault.

When I was ten, he made it possible for the queen of England to know my name.

At twelve, when I was crying, thinking I'd cut myself in an unspeakable place, he held me close and wept with me.

When I was sixteen, he convinced the doctors into believing that I was more important than my infected uterus.

When I was seventeen, he introduced me to Shelley and Byron and Keats and Eliot.

But life is a freak show, and I am stuck playing the role of a good wife.

"Please forgive me," Amir told me last week, "I am powerless. I can't hurt my parents. I'm their only son.... But I promise I'll take good care of you. You'll get your own apartment in another part of the town, or, if you want, I can send you abroad. How does New York sound? If you want a divorce, that can be arranged, too. You're an attractive woman, and you can easily remarry and restart a new life…"

I listened to his generous words and thought to myself: *'You fool, I am not a woman. Don't you see? Knives don't cut me. Your mother's words can't touch me. Your pathetic excuses and your sacrificial voice don't melt me. I am glad I don't have a son like you. I am glad I am nobody's mother.'*

This morning, my father told me he'd be here tomorrow, to rescue me from this house of grief. He called me his pretty daisy, cruelly plucked. Is a flower without a carpel a flower at all?

This morning, when I heard my father cry, my heart broke into a thousand pieces. My heart—being snatched and squeezed out dry and smashed against my skull like a crystal glass—did not beat anymore when my father hung up the phone.

Therefore this morning, when I heard Amir's mother, screaming at the top of her lungs, I felt nothing.

"Is the Maharani still on the phone with that crafty father of hers?" she asked her son. "What evil plan is he cooking this time, I wonder! That man has a PhD in how to marry off a useless daughter to a decent man without paying a single dime as a dowry. What a deceitful man!"

Because the morning was already blank and no words of hers

were big enough to fill my void, I decided to echo her scream.

"Dear mother-in-law of mine," I stood in front of her and snapped, "mark my words. From now on if any bitch or her son tries to insult my father, I will tear their tongue off and feed it to the stray dogs." I then walked back to my room like one glorious queen. '*Fucking shit! Now, that's a darn good way to end a circus,*' I told myself as I broke into a laughter.

Dhaka is flooded with people. People walking. People riding—buses, cars, cabs, rickshaws, and bikes. There's light everywhere. Music everywhere. Beggars everywhere. Thousands of them. The moment a car stops at a traffic light, beggars swarm around it like bees. "Give me a few bucks, my baby is starving." "Give me a few bucks, my baby is dying." "Give me a few bucks, my baby...." These beggars and their problematic babies! The moment someone lowers the car window to drop a few bills, three hands of different sizes would dive in: the raggedy hands of a pregnant mother and her two toddlers. The fourth hand would have joined the trio if only it knew how to dig through the mother's bulging belly. Hundreds of hands then stall cars and block traffic. In the meantime, red becomes green and yellow and then turns red again, while people stay motionless in the stolid wombs of their vehicles, trapped in the vortex of a futile fertility.

Dhaka turns dark almost every night and surrenders its silence to the generators that groan like hungry monsters, gorging on gallons of gasoline. I was thinking of gasoline when the power went off this evening. A few gallons can run a generator all night long. When the house went dark, I left my room and ran through the stairs of a dead house to the moonlit rooftop, where I've spent most of my ten years prison time—nurturing greeneries in potting soil imprisoned in planter cells. Here, I've spent countless nights—hiding away from all the groaning machines and whining humans. But tonight I will not hide. Tonight I am thirsting for fire. Tonight, I have climbed the stairs to stand under a bright sky and fill myself with its vibrant void. And I have brought with me a gasoline can.

The night sky in Dhaka is always lighted. The potted night jasmine shrub always blooms fragrant stars. Gasoline always burns. And my body stands like an eager wick. Tonight, I will plunge into the starry night and pierce through the womb of moonlight like a raging fire. I am not Keats, and loving in half or living in fractions is not my thing. My heart does not ache and my senses never go numb in pain. So, darkling, I listen to the music of my night jasmines. I soak my senses with gasoline and light my bonfire. I kick the dying world one more time before flying away like a blazing phoenix, burning, burning, burning. Burning.

MAKE ME
YOUR SITAR

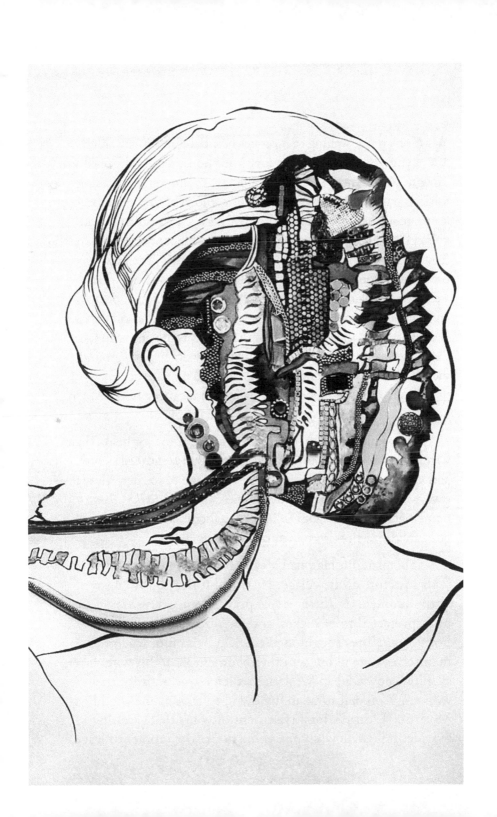

I

Motijan was waiting to meet her new daughter-in-law. Her youngest son, Mafiz, had returned home after eight years and brought with him a new wife. Motijan sat on the veranda, taking tobacco puffs from a hookah. The thick smoke of the cured tobacco leaves itched her throat but calmed her nerves. Her husband had gotten her into this habit of smoking. Every night after dinner, they used to sit in the veranda and smoke together. The man passed away long ago, but his hookah remained with her—like a comforting blanket. Shamsuddin Haq had been a great doctor and a good husband, too. He had given her seven handsome sons. Because of him, she was known in the village as the one with the fortunate womb. New brides and pregnant women from around the village came to seek her blessing. She had to place her hand on their heads and chant repeatedly: "May you mother a hundred sons . . . may you mother a hundred sons . . . may you . . ."

It was not only the pregnant ones who came for help. There were others, too. Women who suffered from physical ailments and women who were broken—they all came to see her. Motijan gave everyone what they needed: a piece of good advice, some homemade remedies, a list of herbal medicines, or a moment of peaceful distraction from their own chaotic lives.

Shamsuddin Haq had always been intrigued by the faith structure of the village. He called it the philosophy of the simpletons. These people prayed to goddess Mansa to be protected from snakes, and to Allah to be protected from Satan. They sought medical help from him when they themselves were ill but sent their womenfolk to his wife. It was as if his knowledge in Western medicine was unfit for their women. "You defeat me in my own profession," he would tell Motijan. "I fear the hungry serpent of yours that's waiting outside. It'll swallow up my whole house the moment I leave."

By serpent, he meant the ever-winding queue of young and old women—coiling around the big jackfruit tree outside the main gate and spreading its tail as far as the road—waiting to be saved. The serpent swerved and swayed, making path for the revered doctor to pass through. They respected the doctor, but it was Motijan they trusted. Shamsuddin Haq knew that it was not Motijan's healing power that brought these women to her. They came because they were drawn to the spark that glowed in her eyes and the fire that lit up into a smile to comfort them. Had he not been married to Motijan, he could be jealous of this ability of hers, the doctor used to say.

"I'm the one who should be jealous," Motijan remembered telling him once. "You have no idea how much they admire you. They say you're the great magician who had saved me from the troubles of raising daughters."

Even though her husband brushed off the compliment with a gracious smile, Motijan knew it to be true. She felt indebted to him for providing her with the power of such motherhood. Motijan firmly believed that women's contentment depended on the strength of men. She never considered herself strong, nor did she believe in the existence of any such woman who might have the courage to stand up without holding the supporting hands of a man. Audacity in a woman was the last thing Motijan ever wished to see.

II

When Shamsuddin Haq got his job as the Chief Surgeon of a government hospital in East Bengal, he left Motijan and the children in Kolkata with her family, promising to send for them soon. But when he did not return in two years, Motijan decided to go in search of him. Her brothers tried to reason with her but she stayed firm in her decision. "Maybe he's fallen ill, or maybe the war has killed him," she told them, "but I need to know for sure."

In the summer of 1916, Motijan arrived on a bullock cart with her two little sons and two handmaids. Shamsuddin Haq was preparing for bed when he heard a constant banging at his door. He thought his house was under attack. Then he heard the familiar voice of a woman, threatening him:

"Are you going to open the door, or should we break in?"

"Good thing I wasn't asleep," he told her as he let her in. "I'd have thought I heard you in my dream and wouldn't have opened the door."

"I know how to break doors," she told him.

That year, Motijan got pregnant with her third son. She became pregnant again the following year, and the year after that. Soon, her new home was full of children and happiness. Once in a while she got homesick and wanted to visit her home in West Bengal.

"We will go very soon, dear," her husband always reassured her. "We will visit them once the war ends. Do you see that river yonder? They live right on the other side, remember? All we'll have to do is cross that river by boat, once the war ends."

Wars ended and began and then ended again. But Motijan never got to cross that river. By the time all her sons grew up, her husband had passed away and her home on the other side of the river had become a part of another country. After her husband's death, Motijan devoted most of her time to her female visitors, giving out blessings and preparing herbal medicine. At night, she sat amidst a crowd of grandchildren—mostly granddaughters, fifteen to be exact, and five grandsons—who rested around her, listening to her stories and waiting for goodnight kisses.

Her daughters-in-law were afraid of her. They believed her to be the cause of their unfortunate pregnancies and blamed her for not giving them her true blessings. Molina, Mafiz's first wife, was the one to openly complain:

"I think she secretly casts spell on us so that we only give birth to girls," she told her husband. "She doesn't want us to have sons."

Pregnant with her first child, Molina became so paranoid that she started avoiding Motijan altogether. "Let's sell this house and move away far from here," she kept telling her husband. "I don't want to be anywhere near her as long as I live!"

Molina's paranoia grew worse during her last trimester. She stayed up all night and hardly ate anything. Mafiz finally decided to let Molina stay with her parents until the baby was born.

When Molina died giving birth to her daughter, Mafiz came back with the newborn and handed it to Motijan. "Do whatever you want with it," he told his mother and left the village. Because Mafiz went missing for a long time, the family almost forgot about him. And because little Alima had no memories of her father, she did not miss him. When Mafiz returned, he expressed the same indifference to his family and showed no interest in the daughter he had deserted eight years ago. He went to see Motijan and spoke casually—about the repair works needed on his old house and about his new job as the head cleric in their local mosque. "By the way, I got myself another wife," he said in a manner of concluding the conversation. "She's waiting in your room to receive your true blessing."

Motijan put down her hookah and went in, not knowing how to react to all the drama that awaited her.

III

Motijan's room was already swarming with people—
women and children—of her own household and from all
around the village. They were excited to hear the news of
Mafiz's return. Nothing exciting ever happened in these remote
villages. Here farmers spent their time tilling their lands and
then their wives, and taking care of their cattle but not of
their wives. Here the women took care of their husbands and
children and not of each other. Here children spent their days
enjoying the innocence of childhood, unprepared to brace all
the upcoming adversities of life. The return of a missing man
with a new bride was therefore a thrilling event for everyone.

Motijan pushed through the curious crowd to unveil the
face of the bride for her visitors. The new bride sat on a corner of
Motijan's huge mahogany bed. Her body, wrapped in a red sari
with her head covered in a long piece of crimson muslin, looked
like a bundle of firewood. Motijan lifted the veil and stood there,
aghast. The girl could not be more than thirteen. Her thirty-one-
year-old son had brought home a child bride.

"She's so young!" someone exclaimed in utter
amazement.

"He surely got himself an untainted fruit," another
woman giggled.

"Isn't she almost Alima's age?" whispered another woman.

"Alima, come meet your stepmother," someone shouted.

"She's not my mother. She's just a little girl." Alima
started crying.

But the women in the room did not pay attention to
Alima. They were busy creating a commotion around the new
bride. If one woman lifted her veil, another placed it back

over her head. If one called her a little girl, another started describing the process by which girls were transformed into women by their husbands. If one called her pretty, another called her plain in comparison to the dead first wife. They kept talking about Molina's tragic death, and about Alima's impending misfortune. "Poor girl lost her mother at birth and got her father back today, only to lose him again," one of the women remarked and the rest of the room sighed in chorus.

The new bride sat perplexed amidst the hubbub, listening to the endless chatter. Clad in a sari and hidden under a long veil, the exhausted girl prayed to God to send an angel with a glass of water and a plate of rice and fish.

"Come, get your mother-in-law's blessing," someone addressed the bride and helped her step down from the bed.

Motijan was sitting in a corner of the room. The bride bowed down to touch her feet. Motijan clenched her jaw as she stood up from her chair and lightly placed her hand on the girl's head.

"Okay, okay, be a mother of a hundred sons," she said abruptly. "Now go—to your room." Motijan then hastily moved away as far as she could—as if any more interaction with the new bride might put her in danger. Suddenly she was angry with the heartless parents of this child bride, with her irresponsible son, and mostly with her dead husband for leaving her with the duty of cleaning up everybody's messes.

IV

The following morning, Mafiz came to her room carrying the unconscious body of his new wife.

"Mother, I have married a possessed woman. Her jinn flew her to the top of the banyan tree last night. See if you can fix her." He dropped the girl by her feet and left.

Motijan used her cane to lift up the girl's sari to find lines of dried blood between her legs. She asked the maids to bring a bowl of rose water and a piece of sandalwood, some warm food and a big mug of tea. She chanted a few verses from the Koran and blew three breaths softly into the bowl. She then sprinkled the water on the girl's face and hair and held the fragrant sandalwood in front of her nose. The girl slowly stirred. She looked at Motijan for a brief moment and then covered her eyes with her hands. She lay in Motijan's lap like a wounded animal. Her little body shuddered and her eyes shed silent tears. Motijan held the girl tightly, allowing her to tremble out the shock. But after a while, as her patience ran out, she addressed the girl in a stern voice:

"Hey, girl, get up and eat something."

The girl sat up and looked crossly at Motijan.

"My name is not girl," she snapped.

"I say finish your tea!" Motijan said again.

"No. I won't listen to you until you call me by my name and ask me nicely."

"Don't you talk back to me, missy!" Motijan said angrily. "I have granddaughters who are older than you, and they never dare raise their voice at me!"

"I'm not talking back! I'm just asking you to call me by my name!"

"Okay then. Tell me your name."

"Rokeya. But I go by Bala," said the girl.

"Fine. Bala, get up and drink the tea."

Bala pulled a stool and sat right across from Motijan. She

took the cup from her hand and started taking little sips.

"My throat hurts from all the crying," she spoke after a while.

"You'll be okay." Motijan tried to sound convincing.

The two women sat quietly and drank their tea, listening to the world outside the room bursting in an uproar.

"What's going on there?" Bala asked.

"My son, your husband, is cutting off the banyan tree."

"Is your son afraid of trees?"

"What made you climb the tree at the dead of the night?" Motijan couldn't help asking.

"I was choking and needed some fresh air."

"So you climb trees when you need fresh air?"

"Why not? Trees bring us air, don't they? And when air gets stuck, all you need to do is shake the topmost branch of a tree to let it free."

The girl looked directly at Motijan as she spoke and smiled with confidence.

Motijan was speechless. For no apparent reason, she felt a stream of fear running inside her veins, like an inviting yet impassable river.

V

For the next few months, Bala slept in Motijan's bed. She played all day with Alima—her stepdaughter—and with Motijan's other grandchildren. At night, she slept like a little kitten in the huge mahogany bed, wrapping her arm around Motijan's flabby waist. At first, Mafiz did not object to the sleeping arrangement. But after a few months, he barged into

Motijan's room one night and forcefully dragged Bala with him to his quarter on the other side of the courtyard.

"Leave her alone! I said, let her go!" Motijan rushed to help.

"Mother, don't come between a man and his wife. You'll burn in Hell, if you do," Mafiz hissed in response.

Motijan walked away in disgust. After that night, she stayed quiet every time Mafiz came for Bala. Then she pretended to be in a deep sleep when Bala returned at dawn, broken and disheveled. When Bala lay down beside her, shaking like a slaughtered lamb, Motijan still kept her eyes firmly closed, as if she were somewhere else, lost in a labyrinth of peaceful sleep.

Sometimes Bala did not return right away. Motijan could hear Bala's footsteps, going in the direction of the pond outside the house. There was a big tamarind tree by the pond. Because Mafiz cut down the banyan tree, Bala walked all the way to the pond to climb the tamarind tree. From her room, Motijan could hear Bala's voice loud and clear—sometimes singing melodious songs, sometimes screaming gibberish, and sometimes laughing nonstop—shattering night's silence into a thousand pieces. But by the time she returned to bed, Bala was back to normal. And in the morning, she acted calm and composed, ready to perform the duties of a responsible stepmother.

Like everyone else in the house, Alima was always curious about Bala's nightly adventures.

"How do you do it?" Alima asked Bala one morning.

"Do what?"

"Climbing. Why aren't you scared of the night?"

"Because I'm not," Bala said.

"But who taught you how to climb so high? Who made you so brave?" Alima asked, unconvinced of her answer. "Tell me, little Mother," she pleaded. "Why do you climb trees at night?"

"It makes me do it," Bala suddenly blurted out.

"Who?" Alima asked.

"Someone I trust."

"But who?" Alima asked again.

"A hand."

"Whose hand?"

"I don't know," Bala replied. "I first saw it the night I came to this house. When I was coming out of your father's room, I heard a rustling sound as if something was trying to sneak in. Then I saw the hand emerging through the door, waving at me. It moved from left to right as if it was trying to—I don't know—either warn me, or invite me into its world. I followed that hand and climbed the banyan tree that night."

Bala paused to catch her breath. Alima shuddered and sat closer.

"Whose hand was it?"

"I don't know. I don't see the rest of the body. Sometimes I imagine it to be a woman—a woman with strong arms and dark eyes—with dreadlocks flowing everywhere, like the monsoon wind. I can smell her presence, you know. Hers is the scent of sandalwood. The moment I smell it, I know I have to be away and free. I follow that scent, and people call it climbing. Sometimes I follow the sound of her irresistible laughter. I smile back at her, and people call it screaming. Her strong fingers play strings of wind, inviting me to sing; but when I sing, people come after me and pull me down from my tree."

"How do you know the hand belongs to a woman? It could be a man's hand, no?" Alima asked.

"It could be, but I don't consider it to be a man."

Alima was suspicious. "But what if it is? I'm sure it's a man's hand," she said persistently. "Only a man's hand would have the courage to be out at night like that. And it's a sin for us to talk to men, isn't it?"

"Everything's sin; or maybe sin is nothing," Bala muttered. "Your father knows these things better, being the head cleric of the mosque. But I don't think such a hand can belong to any man. It just can't."

"You make no sense to me," Alima said.

Being only five years younger than her stepmother, Alima treated Bala like a playmate and never believed anything she said. Therefore, one night, when Bala went to climb her tree, Alima decided to follow.

The house was asleep and the world was still dark. Bala was talking to herself intermittently and humming in an almost uncanny tune. As she reached the tree, Bala turned around and looked right at Alima. She then broke into a laughter, as if she knew all along that she was being followed. She looked at Alima and spread her arms.

"Come with me, little woman, come climb with me to the top of the tree. You'll be fearless forever and you'll be free."

Alima gave out an almost inhuman howl and ran to her father's room. She tried to explain what she saw, but instead fell to the ground, unconscious.

VI

By the time Motijan finished her morning prayer, the inner courtyard was packed with people. She could see all her daughters-in-law standing amidst the gathering. But Bala was not there. Motijan grabbed her cane and walked toward the crowd. She found Mafiz standing outside his house. The door was locked from within and someone was speaking in a nasal voice from inside the room.

"Why are you standing there, Mafiz? Where's your wife?" she hollered at her son.

But Mafiz seemed unresponsive to his surroundings.

"Where is Bala? What have you done to her?" Motijan asked again.

"Keep quiet, Mother! Let the wise man do his job," Mafiz said curtly.

"What wise man? What do you mean?"

Mafiz did not answer. He was paying attention to the wise man's words:

"Spread your legs, you whore," the man said to someone. "Let's see how you like it when I shove these hot red chili peppers in you! If you're a female jinn, then the peppers will give you the pleasure you deserve. If you're a male, then get ready for your punishment. I'll cast a spell so strong that your balls will roll out of your sack and explode! Do you know who I am? I'm Hikmat, the invincible exorcist! The mere mention of my name drove Lord Mountbatten sahib from this country five years ago. Do you know how I punish the cowards like you who hide inside a woman's cunt? I will—"

Motijan could not hear any more. She walked up to the door, but Mafiz moved faster and grabbed her hand before she could knock.

"He's trying to free Bala from her jinn! Don't interrupt him!" Mafiz said.

Motijan pushed Mafiz away and knocked.

"Come out Hikmat the invincible, before I burn this house down! On the count of five," she screamed.

"Mother, are you out of your mind? Do you know what she did last night? She almost killed Alima!"

Mafiz tried to pull her away from the door, but Motijan was blind with rage. She waved her cane at the crowd, pointing it at random faces and screaming at the top of her voice:

"Why are you standing here? You're waiting for a showdown? Here, I'll give you one!"

She walked to the kitchen and brought a lighter and a kerosene container.

"Let's burn all the jinns and demons living in this house for good, shall we?" she said in a calm voice as she knocked at the door again.

"Whon ins scriimmmin there?" the man spoke from inside the room.

"Come out, you hyponasal fraud, and see for yourself. Come out right now, or I will burn you alive!"

"Mother, go to your room!" Mafiz yelled.

"On the count of five, I said. One… two… " Motijan poured some kerosene around the door.

"What are you doing, Mother! This is my house, and she's my wife! You have no right…no right!"

"Three…"

"Someone, come help me carry her away from here. Ouch! Mother! Stop hitting me with your cane!"

"Four…"

"Don't ignite that fire, I'm warning you, Mother!"

"Five!"

The exorcist sprinted out of the room and fell down, rolling on the grass, hiccupping and vomiting foamy bubbles.

"Look at the wise man! He has sucked the evil jinn from Mafiz's wife! Now he's throwing it out," someone said in a satisfied tone.

Motijan rushed inside the room and closed the door behind her. She found Bala lying on the floor. Her nostrils were stuffed with two smoked red chili peppers. Her long hair was braided and wrapped around her neck, like a rope. Her head and her whole face were smeared in red chili paste. Her bare breasts had bruises and burn marks all over them. Her belly button looked like a bowl of red peppers. Her hands were tied behind her back. Her legs, flung open like a forked log, were tied as far apart from each other as possible, and the hollow crack at the juncture was filled with chili paste. Motijan sat beside Bala and took out the chili peppers from her nostrils. She wiped off the paste from Bala's face and freed her neck from the hair-noose. She untied Bala's limbs and emptied the protruded belly button. She used her three fingers to scoop out the paste from inside the unconscious body. Motijan worked unflinchingly with her two big hands, as if those were the only useful limbs a woman needed at that time, or any other time, in order to save someone from drowning.

Motijan asked the maids to carry Bala off to the bathing pond. The crowd had already left. Only Mafiz was there, sitting on a bench by the kitchen. Motijan walked slowly toward her room. Her hands were burning but her heart was numb. She felt drained of all energy. But the moment she saw Mafiz, she lost control:

"Son of Satan!" she screamed. "What kind of a man lets his pregnant wife suffer like this? Swear upon Allah, I will kill you with my bare hands if you even raise a finger at that girl, ever again!"

"She is my wife," Mafiz said.

His face was cold, but his jaws gritted. His nostrils flared, and his eyes looked alert. He sat hunchbacked, with his hands placed on his knees. But his shoulders stuck out, like an animal getting ready to attack its prey. How did she carry this creature inside her womb for nine whole months and nurture him with so much love? Motijan suddenly felt filthy to the core of her bones and rushed toward the bathing pond. She needed a long bath.

VII

Five months later on a stormy night, Bala's water broke. Motijan sent for the midwife and ordered the maids to prepare the birthing room. She gave Bala a warm glass of milk and asked her to finish it before entering the labor room. But Bala refused to go alone.

"I won't go to that grimy room unless you come with me," she said.

"Will you ever learn your lesson? You're too defiant to be a woman, let alone a mother!" retorted Motijan.

"I don't care what you say, but I'm telling you, I'm not going there without you." Bala sat resolute.

Motijan held Bala's hand and helped her walk through the storm, to the dismal room.

The birthing room was an old bamboo house that stood alone by the farthest corner of the backyard. Five of Motijan's seven sons were born there. She had had to enter that room with the first sign of contraction and stay there three weeks after the birth until her body was clean. No one held her hand while she lay in that room, screaming and crying and begging the Almighty to relieve her from the pain. When her sons got married, she never bothered to worry about their wives every time they had their turn to enter that delivery room. She wanted them to experience her pain. And her loneliness, too.

As the midwife began preparing for the delivery, Motijan sat down on the floor and started chanting verses from the Koran.

"Recite sura Ayatul Kurs, dear girl," she told Bala. "Pray to Allah and He will rid you of all dangers. Repeat the sura after me: Allahu la ilaha illa huwal hay-ul Qyuayoom. La taa khuzuhu sinatuwu walanawum…. Now repeat what I said, repeat," Motijan kept pleading.

Bala lay quietly on the reed mattress, biting her lips, in an effort to swallow her pain. She repeated a few lines of the sura. Then she paused and started humming a song. She constantly kept switching back and forth—from singing to chanting to singing—until she stopped chanting altogether and concentrated on her songs.

"Shhhh, don't sing! Recite the sura. Repeat after me: la huma fissamawati wama fil aard…"

"I want to—I—I—I—will sing—a Tagore song. It'll help me—forget—oooooh—the—pain . . ."

"No, no, no. No singing in a moment like this!" Motijan pressed her hand over Bala's mouth. Bala moved it forcefully and kept pleading to Motijan, asking for her permission to sing one more song.

"Have you ever heard Tagore's songs?" she asked Motijan. "Do you want me to sing one for you?"

Without waiting for an answer, Bala then began to sing in a melodious voice:

Pick me up in your strong hands, dear

And make me your sitar.

The magical touch of your fingers
Will bring harmony in the strings
Of my life. Make me strong
With your soft touch, dear,
And make me your sitar.

Motijan started crying. She kept on reciting all the verses she could remember from the Koran. And inside her head, she kept praying for this hopelessly strong girl who held her hand in a tight clasp and kept singing—as if nothing mattered any more.

"Allah, help this wretched girl; Allahu la ilaha illa huwal hay-ul Qyuayoom. There's no God but He—the living and the self subsisting . . ."

Motijan kept reciting and praying and listening to the heart-wrenching song with indivisible attention.

Outside the desolate room, the monsoon storm was taking its toll—on the mango and jackfruit trees, the mud houses, the thirsty fields, and ravenous ponds—with a violent urge to destroy and revive everything anew.

Inside, in the midst of a song and a sura, a fifteen-year-old woman gave birth to a boy who might make her strong and happy with his soft smile. Some day.

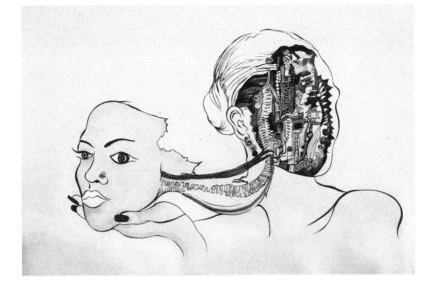

THE BIRD
CATCHER

Part 1: The Bird Catcher

How difficult is the thorny way of strife
That man hath stumbled in since time began,
And in the tangled business of this life
How difficult to play the part of man. (Mirza Ghalib[1])

Once upon a time that was smitten in the dust of dried-out rivers of a fly-swarmed dungeon, there lived—no, breathed—or, more than lived and breathed, but hovered—yes, hovered—a bird catcher, on his arched back, with his question-marked legs and his second-bracket arms—there hovered a bird catcher, holding a magnificent bird trap in one of his second-bracketed hands, while dangling with the other bracket an alluring bird cage almost the size of the world he could not see. His legs grew scales, for he waded through the marshy lands all day long, and his feet turned into claws, for he tip-toed on them through the wrinkled roots of tangled trees all night long. His eyes were not meant to see but to squint the light out from the rest of the world so that all winged songs were confined within the fringe of his riveting gander. His nostrils never twitched, but only flared when a falling feather fluffed through the wind. His ten eyes, five in each hand, one in each fingertip, shone like moonbeams stuck on a frozen surface of what was once a river. And every time he caught any of those wind riders, the surface cracked as he let the birds rest on the hollowness carved inside his palm. Disjointedly, and then en masse, he stroked the feather of those wings of song with his eyes—ten of them—and felt what they felt when touched by the icy coldness hidden underneath his fingertips.

---

1   Most of the poems are quoted from The Hindustani Lyrics, translated by Inayat Khan and Jessie Duncan Westbrook (London: 1919).

The life he lived was of pure and naked existence. For
him, life meant love of life. He thrived for his needs and
lived for the satiety of them. For him, need was a happy
dependence—an exultant void that must be filled. He always
needed to sink his teeth into things to gratify himself—by
assimilating, absorbing, or negating everything. He believed in
the power of reason, and reason only. For him, reason is what
made everything possible. For him, reason was the master in
control of the beginnings and the ends. The bird catcher was
the master of reason.

The first time he heard the bird, singing its melodious
song and flying over the boundless sky like a rhythm of wings
in motion, the bird catcher felt the need to cage her joyful
spirit. To him, the bird that had the heart to sing immortal
joys was nothing if not owned by him. He thought his life
might lose its purpose until the bird that never alighted sat in
his cage and sang, only for him.

The bird catcher still remembered the day he caught
that beautiful bird. The day always flashed before him like
tomorrow's dream. On that day, the sky cracked into a
thousand pieces and poured itself over barren lands. Lightning
lashed and wind hissed and leaves roared and branches
groaned and trees swooned and rivers swelled, and amidst
the furious gleam of an eternal light, the fervent earth danced
its dance of a thousand veils. Thunderstorms flashed and
flicked through the dense leaves that clutched the intertwined
branches of *ashvattha* and *ashoka* and spruce and fir and pine
and *parijat* trees—all intermingled and clenched like a flock of
perplexed animals in a flooded forest. That day, while hiding
under the disheveled branches of bereaved trees, waiting to
breach the gripping moment that wedged between a rising
squall and a ceasing wind, the bird catcher felt a feather—
fluttering and falling—like an eager leaf. He squinted his
eyes to drain all light from the universe and stretched his

moonbeam fingers upward. He then held his cage tightly with one hand and crawled through the jumbled trees. Like a cautious ant he crawled, and like a hungry armadillo he slouched and sidled in the motion of a silent snake until he reached his bird. The moment his frosty fingers brushed against its feathers, his bird stiffened. The moment his arched hand plucked it like a fruit, his bird muffled and fell like a sun drop. And the moment it fell, there was light everywhere. The world, his world, every inch of his unfathomably grudging world that he carried inside each of his clawed toenails and beneath his perceptive veins, and the world that he caged in his globular crate and squatted on his back—all these worlds were reborn in that light. The bird catcher's deadened eyes glowed with glee as he locked his cage and started his homeward journey.

He had been waiting for years for this bird that never descended. His beard had turned into snow and his skin drew wrinkled lines all over his face while he waited, watching all birds, other birds, this bird—singing and dancing and flying. Moon-bitten and darkness-smeared, he watched those birds as they decorated their dancing ground with sapling sticks and piles of bright berries before spreading their plumes in frantic dance moves. He watched how this bird—his bird—stayed away from all that happened in the forest. She never paused from flying. She circled over and around the dancing ground, spreading her wings like a colorful canopy underneath a starlit sky. Many a time, like Sanggenyawai the Maring, the bird catcher had blackened his body with charcoal to turn his human shape into a Kalanc bird2. He then sat on the top

2   According to a myth popular in the Maring community of Papua New Guinea, Sanggenyawai was a bird catcher and a hunter, who lived in the dense forest with his wife and a little daughter. He kept Kombam and Kalanc birds of paradise as his pet, and hunted Kapul birds for food. One day, enamored by its beauty, Sanggenyawa's brother-in-law killed one of the Kombam birds. Sanggenyawai killed his brother-in-law and made his wife suffer for her brother's crime by deserting her in the forest. Sanggenyawai then grieved for his dead bird by covering his body with charcoal and turning into a Kalanc bird. He then flew away to the forest, never to resume his human life.

branch of the tallest *araucaria* tree, from where he observed this magnificent bird that never alighted; never aroused, never allured, never tempted to be tempted by the irresistible display of plumes. "Only that bird, or no more"—was the promise that the bird catcher had made to himself the day he first saw her. The promise finally came to life as the bird lay stiff in the cage that clinked and clanked to resonate the mirth that muffled the hunter's heart.

* * * *

The bird catcher put his bird in a glorious vault, hidden from all sights and sounds. He served the bird bright berries and red cherries, raisins and nuts. He decorated each plume with diamond studs, placed a pearl around her throat and pinched sapphires on her beak; he put long anklets on both of her feet and secured the other ends of those precious anklets to the door of her elegant cage. Then he hung the cage like a chandelier at the center of the room and walked around it, holding a gorgeous golden whip in his hand, waiting for the heavenly bird to gratify him with her song.

"Sing for me, beautiful bird, sing and dance for me."

He swished his golden whip and chanted as he walked around the cage:

"Sing, beautiful bird, sing for me, and make me the happiest man on earth. I need you to bestow upon me your cherished treasures that are meant to make me strong in will and invincible in spirit."

And for a while, the bird only breathed silence.

"Sing, or I will let you be no more," said the bird catcher, in an utmost anger.

"Let your arrows pierce me and strike me dead," hummed the bird.

"Why don't you sing? Sing! Why don't you dance? Dance! Aren't I the one who owns your gifts by owning you?"

"You are the one who captured me."

"Isn't it true that you are to give your treasures to the man who sees you first?"

"Yes. And that I did."

"Then where are those? I do not seem to find them with me."

"You are the one who captured me. And the one who saw me before you was given his due gifts."

"But how can that be? Before I caught you, I know you were free."

"I was free because I had already given away my gifts," said the bird, "to someone who never needed them."

"If you are my bird, your gifts are mine too!"

"First, tell me this," asked the bird. "Are you serene and calm and unafraid when you consider your tyranny?"

"Why do I need to be otherwise? I am calm and unafraid, and I need to own your cherished gifts. Because you are mine. "

"If you think you need them, then they are not for you. Because you will never comprehend," said the despondent bird.

The bird catcher sat in front of the cage, day after day, waiting to receive his gifts, and the bird that used to sing joyous songs went mute remembering. But when the sun darkened and the stars clouded the sky, and when the bird catcher went to the forest for his hunting game, the bird would stir and dance and softly sing. Away from the sky and adorned with life's shining shackles, she sat alone in the cage and thought of the void of the sky. She imagined flying in that void. And she imagined singing eager songs for some disinclined listener, who could hold freedom in his eyelids the way morning held the night. The bird then sang as if she were living in two different times and two different worlds; as if she had an ardent listener somewhere out in the air —as if the air surrounding her cage were filled with eons of willingness for a melody that was spread from ether to ether—encompassing the endless sky under whose shade lived all the catchers of birds and the holders of freedom.

* * * *

The bird catcher came back one morning to find his bird singing a melodious tune. But the moment he entered the room, the bird lost her song. The moment he approached his bird, the fire of anger that flashed through his relentless gaze scorched her rhythm. The bird closed her eyes and flapped her wings as if to brush off the remnants of her last song from every memory.

"I am sure I heard you sing. Who was that you were singing to?" the bird catcher wanted to know.

"No one," the bird said. "No one that matters to you."

"But who is it that matters to you so much that you change your color and shift your melody—from somber to sonorous, then somber again? Why do you appear happy when I don't see what you see? I want to see," said the bird catcher. "I want to see what and who you see."

"I sing the music of nothingness. When I sing, I see the inside of my head. And there I see a whole universe, where you cannot enter because that is not yours to claim, because it does not belong to me. I sing my somber songs to whom the universe inside me does not belong."

"I want to see your inside," said the bird catcher. "I want that universe. I will have it. They said I could not capture you because you were not to be captured alive, because you fly above and beyond anyone's reach, and you never rest your feet and wings. But when I trapped you in my cage, they said I shouldn't have captured you, for you were too divine a bird to live in my cage, and they said you would bring me death within forty days. It has been thirty winters already, and I am still here, aren't I? And I am sure I will own the universe inside your head one day. What you have, I must own."

"You, my jailor, have exhaled thirty breaths, and you may breathe ten more to complete the number. But what you call a year, I call a fleeting moment trapped between a blink."

"I will pull with my ten fierce fingers what you hide in that fleeting moment of your blink."

The bird catcher suddenly opened the door of the cage and pulled the bird by her wings. He placed her on his left palm and felt her warmth. With his moonbeam fingers, he caressed each plume of his bird from end to end. He pressed his cheek on her beak and nudged his nose in her eyes. With his right index finger he touched the bird's neck, her throat, her back, below her plumage and between her legs. He then used his fingertip eyes to search for the universe that lay hidden in her head. He punched her head open and inserted his fingers, one by one, inside the tiny head in a futile attempt to find a universe that was not his to claim. He plunged his thirsty fingers into the bird's chest and then pulled her apart, plume-by-plume, pore-by-pore, shredding her skin and crushing her bones, searching for a soul that was never his to seek.

"Talk to me, my bird! Move the tongue that I ripped with my fingers; open your mouth that I thrashed with my hands; blow air into your windpipe that I so immaculately tore and twisted into a string, which can only move if touched by the gentle breeze passing through it."

O my captor, your words flow like silver torrents. Alas, I have no voice that you can ever hear, sang the bird in a voice that was gone.

For the bird catcher, clarity was not the disappearance of confusion; it was the confusion. Therefore, he never heard the bird when she was there—or when she was not. But songs are meant to be sung and heard, and a song of willingness always reaches the willing soul. That day, when the bird catcher killed the bird, her songs spread in the ether and reached the listener who knew how to hear silence. The listener was a dispassionate hermit who lived in desolation—from the world and its cruelty. Because the listener was not there in the bird catcher's world, the bird always felt his presence in the air and sang for him the songs of her loneliness. And because he had never seen the bird, he could see her clearly; clarity for him was the presence of strength. As the silent song of a perished voice reached him, the lonely listener's reticence was broken by his willingness to be with a bird that was not there anymore. In his eagerness to be with the bird of serenity, the lonely listener had a vision, in which he saw himself being approached by the bird—with promises of impossible possibilities.

"O bird, I know why you are here. Now I will see you dance and hear you sing," said the recluse in a soundless voice, to the bird that was gone.

"But that must not be. You and I live on two ends of the endless string of time," whispered the dead bird in silence.

"But bird, you are free, and I want to be with you! I want you to untie me from my bondage," urged the listener..

"O recluse," said the bird, "in order to be with me, all you have to do is not to be."

"But I am ready—now and hereafter—not to be. But I still cannot see you!"

"You will see me when you are nowhere to be seen. And you will hear my song long after it is over; and you will play my melody on your strings, because your tunes and my songs are nothing but the manifestation of one string."

"But how will I know when not to be?" asked the desperate listener.

"You will know, because I have already left my song for you. You will hear it when the ground beneath your feet will resonate with the rhythm of unending melodies."

The unuttered words of a distant recluse elapsed into the oblivion and the bird that was not there anymore flew away—from the distraught world of the bird catcher, through the abyss of truths—to the rift of memories.

Meanwhile, unable to find the treasures within the body that he had disassembled like the countless puzzle pieces of dismantled dreams, the bird catcher took his cage and his trap and embarked on a journey in search of the three treasures that the bird never gave him. He went to retrace every step that he had taken until he reached the point where he began his search. The treasures must be somewhere by that araucaria tree where he had found her, he thought. Maybe she had dropped her soul in the hollow of the big redwood tree before leaving the second treasure on top of the araucaria. And maybe she left the third one by the Padma River, where he once found her dipping her feathers in the blue water. He had to find them—her soul, her mirth, and the universe that she kept hidden from him—and he would leave no worlds unturned until he owned them. He was a man in search of treasures that he thought were rightfully his, and no mountain was high enough to block his path.

Part 2: The Recluse

O Wind of Disaster, destroy not the home of my heart
With the blasts of thine ire,
For there I have kindled to burn in a chamber apart
My Lamp of Desire. (Amir Minai[3])

Wearied by Monte Rosa's eternal display of snows and glaciers, the bird spread her wings to start a wayward flight and beckoned the mistral wind to follow her track. She scoured her feathers in the shiny sweetness of the Rhône Valley and touched the peak of Beinn Nibheis to quench her thirsting spirit, before landing to rest on a rowan tree that stood like a colossal shadow of life's vestige by the flowing stillness of Loch Awe. She framed the tiny Fraoch Eilean in her eyes and absorbed the calm of Loch Awe in her throat. Beneath her, under the shade of the big rowan tree, sat the recluse for whom she was yet to sing her last song before the bird catcher took away her voice. The recluse had not heard her songs yet, and therefore was not aware of her willing spirit. Looking at his disinterested face, the bird knew this man would never want to capture her, for he showed no emotions of worldly needs. The ones that are driven by their needs do not know what and how to desire—and because they do not know, they crave and claim and live to lust. But this man's face reflected no wrinkles of needs. As if he wanted nothing. As if he knew that the world was not obliged to fulfill his needs. But deep within the darkness of his eyes, the bird saw an immitigable longing—a desire to know, to be known, to accept and to surrender. She felt an urge to surrender her whims to this

---

3   Amir Minai (1828-1900): a famous Urdu poet from Lucknow.

disenchanted hermit—before her miserable future reached her and tarnished her sublime spirit.

The bird sat on a branch of the rowan tree and started singing. But seeing the hermit's undivided attention to the emptiness around him, she went quiet, like a moment frozen beyond time's horizon. Days passed to months, and months vanished into years. The hermit's shadow moved from beneath the tree toward the direction of his broken abode, and to the lake yonder, and then back under the tree. And still the bird sat, watching a human's uncanny absence from his surrounding world. It was as if he did not exist. And yet, it was as if because he existed, nothing else needed to exist, for his was not the existence of need. Behind her two eyes and within her captivating tune, the bird held the knowledge of what was yet to come. And because she knew what was not there yet, she was aware of a bird catcher, who, one day—out of his sheer need of possession—would take away everything from her. Because she could see the time that was yet to come, the bird flew to the time that was already there—a time that the recluse was yet to see—and left a trail of her songs, which one day he was sure to find.

The bird sat on the branch of the rowan tree and watched the man who seemed unaware of her present or his future. But then he spoke one day in a voice colder than Loch Awe's calm.

"Why do you disrupt my world? Are you here to sing? Do not sing for me, Alkonost, Gamayun, Sirin, or whoever you are," he said crossly, "and if you are a Sirin, you must not sing to me, for I was never happy[4]. " The recluse looked up at the tree for a moment, but not at the bird.

"Why don't you like my song, recluse? Haven't you suffered enough, living through your sanctimonious disharmony for so long?" the bird asked.

4   Deriving from the Slavic and Russian folktales, Alkonost, Gamayun, and Sirin are half-bird and half-woman creatures with magical power to mesmerize humans with their enchanting voices.

"Your melody is annoying. And your music is just an infuriating flow of nothingness."

"O recluse, you don't know it yet, but our whole being—yours and mine—is music; our mind and our body, and the nature that is in us, above us, beneath us, and around us, everything is nothing but music."

"I want you to stop singing," said the persistent recluse. "If you are a Huma5, then you must not descend on my rowan tree, for I do not intend to kill you for my happiness."

"I am not singing," said the bird.

"Then what is that I hear? Isn't that your song rustling within the creases of those bursting rowan leaves?"

"That was a song I left for you thirty springs ago. You are only hearing it now."

"I was not here, then," said the recluse. "You cannot leave a song for someone who was not here."

"It took you that long to reach my song. I was singing that song thirty springs ago, right before the bird catcher found me near Mount Kailas."

"What bird catcher? This place is far away from Mount Kailas and too remote for the catchers of birds to travel in search of a bird that never lives on the ground."

"Well, I sang that song then, so that you can hear it now."

"I hear it now."

---

5   Referred as Umay in Turkish mythology, as Homa in Indian mythology, and as Huma and Simorgh in Persian mythology and Sufi fable, the bird is said to have magical and divine power. This mythical bird spends its life flying invisibly high above the earth, and never alighting on the ground.

The Sufi tradition takes the bird as a symbol of spiritual harmony and knowledge. According to Inayat Khan, the renowned Sufi philosopher, Huma is a compound Arabic word of Hu (Spirit) and Ma'a (Water). In Sufi tradition, by catching a glimpse of the bird or its shadow one can attain perpetual happiness and divine power. It is impossible to catch the bird alive, and the person who catches it and thus kills it by doing so, is believed to die within forty days.

"That means I was here then."

"And I can see you now."

"No, you cannot see me, because it's been ten springs since I am gone. The life you think you see is less than a shadow."

"I can see you now, and I am not dreaming."

"No; you don't see me."

"What am I looking at then, if it is not you?"

"What you see now is yesteryear's reality."

"Mark my words, bird. I do not believe in the past anymore; for me, everything is a constant flow of present."

"And yet, what you are calling present belonged to my past and your future."

"No! You make no sense!" The recluse stood up, with his shoulders spread like wings and his hands thrown upward like the stretched end of his wings. "I can see your plumage!"

"Yes, that you will, one day. Now you can see me because you haven't seen me yet. Because I am already gone."

"But why will I want to see you?"

"You will see me because it will be your heart's desire, and because it is my desire. I am but a trace of me in your memory, which you have not gathered yet. And I will store in your memory my most cherished treasures."

"Why are you spreading your wings for me? Are you showing me your colors? I don't want your treasures! Shoo, bird, shoo!"

"Look at me, recluse. Hear me sing and watch me dance. This is my gift of serenity to you."

"O evil bird! Are you trying to tempt me to leave my unhomely home and return to the ruins of life listlessly lingering out there in that forcefully joyous side of the world? Have you any idea how many mountains I have crossed in order to stay away from the seductresses of your kind? Always dancing, always tapping their feet, always surging waves through every curve of their bodies! Oh! Oh!"

"Come close and feel my heartbeat. I am offering you the beating of my ageless heart, long before the bird catcher takes it away."

"What bird catcher? Why do you keep talking about things that are not here? And how can you survive without your heart?"

"It is because of that I will survive, and you will never grow old; so I give you the beating of my ageless heart."

"Shoo, bird, shoo!"

"And I will stay with you through all eternities because Time doesn't frighten you, and that is my third gift."

"Shoo, bird, shoo! Your words are disturbing and your song is annoying." The recluse picked up a dried rowan fruit and threw it in the bird's direction. But there was no bird to be seen anywhere and the leaves of the tree hung silent and unstirred, like the dead thoughts of an unseen future. The recluse closed his eyes to open his ears. But all he could hear was the flow of silence that calmed the gasp of the lake around the broken walls of his ruined castle.

Part 3: The Bird

I cannot rise to follow her,
Here in the dust is my abode,
For I am but her footprint left
Lying forgotten in the road. (Insha6)

The recluse has no memory. For him memories are little maggots that live on dead thoughts. He has shed the life that was once his like a snake sheds its skin. He has grown a new skin, for the old one was soaked in pains and loathing. He was once the slave of his needs. The life that he lived was that of an executioner. All he did was kill, kill, kill, kill, kill, kill. He killed his soul, his body, his conscience, his emotions, his feelings, and his ability to see the truth that always stared right into his eyes. His only source of joy came from the words that he did not, could not speak. The words that he inked and then smudged and inked back again always anchored his drifting heart for a while, and then they let him drift back to his solitude.

The recluse is only moved by a sheer willingness—of desire. In desire, there is no sinking of one's teeth into the flesh of the world, no satiety. Desire is the uncharted future unbounded by needs. To him, separation from himself and from the world is solitude; for him, enjoyment of solitude is happiness. The way night grows accustomed to darkness and the sun grows accustomed to sharing sky's canopy with so many other blind suns and stars, the recluse has grown accustomed to the silence around him. Music annoys him; dancing irritates his eyes; the very thought of listening to a rhythmic heartbeat evokes a death wish

---

6   Insha Khan (1757-1817): a famous Urdu poet and a talented polyglot, he wrote the first book on Urdu grammar and language in 1807.

in him. He does not believe in life, nor does he believe in death. Time is but an illusion to him. Life is nothing but a tiny dot that he endures in order to connect with the next dot and then continue moving forward. Memories have no function for him in this continuum of time, life, or death. Memories are anomalies, if anything at all.

But forty summers ago, one incessantly singing, dancing, talking bird drilled a chasm in the crypt of his thoughts, and allured him to remembrance. He remembers why he did not see the bird when she was there, and he knows why he sees the bird without seeing. He now knows he is nothing but the footprint, which the bird has left behind. He knows he has been to her world, a world full of enticing words and exuberant hues. He remembers how, unlike him, she pushes every word out of her throat and spreads them in the ether, in a ceaselessly harmonious beat—like the rhythmic configurations played on a tabla:

Dha Den Taal Tete Katal Gadi Ghenel

Dha. Den. Taa. Tete. Kata. Gadi. Ghene.

DhaDenTaa TeteKataGadiGhene

Dha . . .

An urge grows in him to set his mind back in rhythm again. As he looks beneath his feet and above his head and beyond his vision, his heart vibrates the desire to submerge in a rhapsody of sound and color.

The earth speaks to him in a vibrant voice. Her pitch is on the surface, her form is crescent-like, and her color is yellow. The dim and dull sound of the earth generates a thrill of movement through his body.

He hears the sound of water, which is turquoise green in color, and which is serpentine in shape; he hears its voice in the roaring of the ocean.

He hears the high-pitched sound of fire, which is curled in form and red in color, and he hears its voice in the thunderbolt.

He hears the wavering sound of air, which is meandering in form and blue in color.

And he finds the sound of ether as self-contained that holds all forms and colors within. It is black and it is white. It is the base of all sounds, and it is the undertone7.

As his heart begins to beat in rhythm, the recluse closes his eyes just so he can forget the colors of the bird's plumage. But instead, his eyes glow like the bird's mirror. As the light inside his eyes bedazzles him, he forcefully opens them to unsee the light within and looks outside into the darkness that veils the earth around him. But there is nothing to see.

* * * *

The bird once told him that if everything else fails, the law of reciprocity would allow him to see what she saw. The recluse closes his eyes again in search of that reciprocity, and when he opens his eyes, he finds himself sitting under the shade of a big Moreton Bay fig, on whose stooping branch hangs a globule that holds the bird that never alights. The sound of his breathing beams like a lingering flow of dreams around the brassbound globule. As he approaches the bird, she closes her eyes because she knows light is nothing but what the darkness reveals.

"Why do you come to me, bird, when I can't see you? Why do I want to be seen by you? Tell me, who am I to you?" the recluse eagerly asks.

---

7 The concept of the presence of sound and color in all elements of Nature is borrowed from Inayat Khan's sound theory of elements, as described in his book, The Mysticism of Sound (1923). Inayat Khan (1882-1927) introduced the Western world to his mystic theory that blended Indian classical music with Sufi tradition.

"Like a wandering melody, I have traveled and floated with the wind, untamed and untaken. I have flown above the clouds of the five oceans and the seven seas. My thirsting soul has dipped in every river that one can name, from Mississippi to Murray. I have drifted from one mountain range to another—from the Andes to the Zagros—and yet, the only place that ever offered me a piece of golden sunshine is the heart that beats in you. The thirst that springs forth from the willing heart of yours is what you are to me," the bird does not say.

* * * *

The recluse starts his mountain-bound journey in order to be found by the bird. When he reaches Mount Kailas, he sees the endless patch of fir and spruce and pine trees stooping as if to mourn a loss. Their branches are shrouded with snow and their trunks are covered in blood. Somehow he knows something has died somewhere, but he does not know what it is. His agony drives him to the mountain peaks and he tries to hide his pain in barren wilderness; sometimes he sits by the evening tide, and sometimes he rises with the sun and then watches it sink into the evening ocean, while he waits for a song. Then he resumes his journey anew, wading through the rivers—from the Ganges to the Iravati, and walking through the mountains—from Karakush to Kilimanjaro, seeking a bird that he thinks is seeking him. Sore at heart and drained of hope, he sits under a giant kapok tree, wishing without knowing what to wish for.

"Are you crying? Why are you crying, recluse?" Suddenly appearing from behind the clouds that lurk over the kapok tree, the bird flies around the lonely man and starts asking him questions that he only can answer with more questions.

"O bird, are you the thorn among the thorns, a rose among the roses, a thought among thoughts, and a sorrow among my sorrows?" the recluse asks. "You are never mine and you never will be, for I cannot have you. And yet, why does it hurt when I think of losing you? I do not want to lose you."

"You will never lose me for that very reason, recluse; because I was never yours to claim."

"Is this love? This feeling that thuds inside me like the beat of my heart and then surpasses the flow of my blood—is this what love feels like? Do I want you because I love you?" The hapless hermit wants to know in earnest.

"What you feel is more than love," says the bird. "Without love, we can live; but without willingness, we are nothing. What you feel is the willingness to surrender to whose existence you have never been aware of, and to whom you may be nothing more than a blade of grass she may never tread on. It is your willingness to surrender to this other— to her perceived universe and to her sense of existence and annihilation—that drives your heart and makes you different from all the bird catchers of the world. This feeling is therefore not love, but knowledge. Love demands fulfillment of needs, and yours is not a need. What you feel is what you are."

The bird knows what the recluse does not: birth and death and the interval that stands in between are bound by nothing but pure thought. She has flown from time past— where nothing is possible anymore—to the time to come— where every possibility is pending. She has seen the memories that recapture and reverse the passivity of what once was and what still remains. Because she knows that memories are what pains are made of, and because she wants the recluse to be untouched by her pains, the bird has once again flown over the strings of time, hoping to replace her past gifts with a new song of pure thought. She knows that to sing is to make the invisible visible, the impossible possible, and to feel at home in a world where no one belongs.

"I urge you to give me back the three metaphors that I once bequeathed to you," says the bird.

"Which metaphors?"

"I gave you the power to see the unfading color of my plumage. My gift of serenity. I want it back."

"No."

"I handed you the beat of my heart, my gift of eternal youth; and I now want it back."

"No."

"I promised to be your companion of all worlds and none. I want you to give me back my promise."

"No."

"Why not?"

"Why do you want them back?"

"Because, recluse, you are not meant to be the one to have them, not anymore."

"Why? What changed?"

"Nothing ever changes in this world of yours that is bound by time and need. Time frightens you and you always divide it into three. And you, recluse, are still haunted by the guilt of your ruthless needs—still devoid of pure thought."

"I refuse to give them back."

"But why won't you return them?"

"Because, dear bird, I never return what I am given."

"Oh, no, no, no, no! Please, do not say that! Aren't you a poet, recluse? Aren't you aware of the power that lies hidden within one's metaphors? They are my life's treasures; in fact, they are my life. What will you do with them?"

"If they are metaphors, then they are mine as much as they are yours."

"But why do you want them now? Why do you want what is not, what cannot be, and what will never be? What will you do with them? They are nothing to you; but they are my everything. Those were nothing but the whims of a bird that was never meant to descend. I danced for you, recluse, in a whimsical spree, I spread my wings for you and descended inside your head; my whims are gone now, and I want my metaphors back, for I do not want you to suffer for an unearned loss. They are not real, recluse, they never were."

"Then fear not, bird, for I do not believe in reality. I do not believe in life or death anymore. I only believe in the eternal flow of time. You and I, we are eternally connected to this endless flow of time. You and I, bird, you and I are inseparable."

"What will you do with them? Why do you need me?"

"I don't need you, but I cannot do without you. You and I are, because we are meant to be. We could have done nothing to stop this fate. What is done is done."

"I will chase you from one universe to another, from one galaxy to the next, from one life to many thereafter, until you give me back my metaphors."

"And still I will refuse to give them. The only way you can have them back is by snatching them forcefully."

"How can I take back what you refuse to give? Am I to be the plunderer of my own dreams? O recluse, you are a cruel, cruel man, even more unkind than the one who was once my jailor! I promise I will not stop chasing you until you give them back."

"Then I will never give them back, for I do not want to

lose you."

"O recluse, I wish I had never descended on your rowan tree. You have shackled me with my own treasures. And now, you and I are bound to meet when all that is limited is effaced to the limitless perpetuity."

To the recluse, the bird's words seem like a whirlwind of circuitous thoughts. But he knows why whirlwinds happen. Filled with an unending longing, the recluse awaits to be beaten and tossed and absorbed and dismantled by the reckless uniformity that belongs to a perplexing world of the timeless bird. He stretches his hands to let the whirlwind in. But the bird has flown away, chanting a tune of despair.

* * * *

The recluse finds himself in a shifting room of mirrors, at the center of which stands an empty earthen cage carved in the shape of a bird that he has been seeking. He walks in the garden in search of the bird and rests under a big *parijat* tree. The rustling wind brushes against the fragile blooms and pours them gently on his lap. He stoops down to pick up a handful of flowers, only to find a soft and slender plume. The recluse picks up the feather and brushes it against his cheek. The soft feather trembles as he touches it with his lips and lets its warmth linger over his eyes. The willowy feather stirs as if turned back to life by a mere touch, as the hand that holds it quivers like a bird. But his legs grow strong and restless, for they suddenly remember wherein lies the path to serenity.

His heart than rises and follows his feet. Time is but ripples of memory, and space, its molted shadows. Floating as a pair of lotus leaves, his feet walk through the ripples and the shadows to reach where the oceans meet the highest of mountains. He walks right into the juncture of earth and sky, where the color of the roaring wind meets the sound of the

fading sun. The plume of his lost bird that once stirred in
his hand and trembled at his touch now stops shivering. He
takes up the delicate feather and lets it gently glide through
his slender neck. The ocean rises to pull the mountains down
with her and the sky collapses over the mountains, while
the recluse stands unmoved like a shadow of Beinn Nibheis,
watching his dewdrop life disappear in the endless ocean of
time. The recluse closes his eyes and smiles the way a day or a
sun or a moon or a god of all gods smiles. He smiles because
now he knows that a thinking thought is only a moment of
reconciliation, not freedom: it is a moment when the eternal
flow of possibility that is hidden in a thought is reduced to
reality. The recluse surrenders all his thinking thoughts to an
illimitable longing for one pure thought, yet to arrive.

"O, Bird of spirit and water, everywhere I look, I see your face

Everywhere I go, I arrive at your dwelling place

In search of you I pass away into nothingness.

I vanish—and I am all living again."

The recluse smiles because he is free. When time is
indivisible, one will never cease to be.

About the Artist

Chitra Ganesh graduated magna cum laude from Brown University in with a BA in Comparative Literature and Art-Semiotics, and received her MFA from Columbia University in 2002. For over a decade, Ganesh's work has been widely exhibited both locally and internationally, including at the Queens Museum, Museum of San Diego LA Jolla, Berkeley Art Museum, Bronx Museum, Pennsylvania Academy of Fine Arts, and Baltimore Museum. International venues include Fondazione Sandretto (Turin), the Saatchi Museum (London), MOCA Shanghai, Kunsthalle Exnergrasse (Vienna), and Kunstverein Gottingen (Germany) with solo presentations at PS 1/MOMA, the Andy Warhol Museum, Brooklyn Museum, and Gothenburg Kunsthalle (Sweden). Ganesh's work is widely recognized in South Asia, and has been shown at The Indira Gandhi National Centre for Arts (New Delhi), Princes of Wales Museum (Mumbai), Devi Art Foundation (New Delhi), Travancore Palace (New Delhi) and the Dhaka Art Summit at Shilpakala Academy (Bangladesh). She has been named Robina Foundation Fellow for Arts and Human rights at Yale University Law School (2015-16), US Art in Embassies Program resident in NIROX, South Africa (2015), Estelle Lebowitz Endowed Visiting Artist (2015); Kirloskar Visiting Scholar at RISD (2014), and Artist-in-Residence at New York University's Asian/Pacific/American Studies Program (2013-14). She has also has held residencies at the Lower Manhattan Cultural Council, Headlands Center for the Arts, Smack Mellon Studios, and the Skowhegan School of Painting and Sculpture. Ganesh has received numerous grants including a John Simon Guggenheim Fellowship in the Creative Arts (2012), and awards from the Art Matters Foundation (2010), Joan Mitchell Foundation (2010), New York Foundation for the Arts (2009), and New York Community Trust (2006), among others. Her works are held in prominent public collections such as the Philadelphia Museum of Art, San Jose Museum of Art, Baltimore Museum, the Whitney Museum, and Museum of Modern Art. Ganesh has most recently been awarded a Hodder Fellowship for the 2017-18 academic year at Princeton University's Lewis Center for the Arts. Learn more at www.chitraganesh.com